The Beautiful Life of Sofia

The Beautiful Life of Sofia

Margaret Azzinaro-Bonacci

ISBN-13: 9781512055191
ISBN-10: 1512055190

The Beautiful Life of Sofia is a work of fiction. Names, characters, places, and incidents are the product of the author's imagination. Any resemblance to actual persons, living or dead; events; or locales is entirely coincidental.

Book design by Stacey N Naim

Check Out Our Reviews!

Bravo! Smooth and easy reading. Just loved flipping
the pages!
—AB, Florida

Warm and friendly. An easy ready!
—JC, Jersey City, New Jersey

I cried, I laughed, I couldn't put it down. I want book two!
—Lizzetta, Florida

I couldn't wait to tell her it's wonderful!
—Lori, Boston, Massachusetts

Congratulations—a job well done! I loved every word.
—Chrissy, Middle Village, NY

Cute and heartwarming
—DH, Long Island, NY

I really loved the story. It was so intriguing; it kept my attention throughout the book. I applaud you. I wish you all the best!
—Mary, Brooklyn, New York

To my sons, my life, my loves: Michael, Anthony, and Frank:

Watching you grow has given me so much joy, love, support, and just plain, ordinary good times with lots of laughs. My boys are just the best. In good times and in bad, we are there for one another. Thank you, my sons, for being a blessing in my life.
I hope you enjoy my book.

With much love,

Mother

To my nephew, Justin.

When you were a little boy, I would sit with you for hours and tell you stories; you loved them all. Each passing year, you would ask me, "Aunt Gog, did you ever finish that book?" That day is here; my book is complete. So to you, my dear nephew, Justin, I love you and thank you for always believing in me. Justin, you were so special to Papa, and you have grown into a wonderful young man. You make us all proud.

Thank you for pushing me to the finish line.
All my love,
Aunt Margaret
"Gog"

Writing a book is never easy; I have learned that. The truth is, I needed help. Boy, did I find just the right girl for me! She is smart and loved the book. With her working very hard, side by side with me, hour after hour, I wrote, changed, wrote, and changed some more. It was a tough job. She was dedicated, and I absolutely loved working with her. I could not have finished this book if not for her and all her help. She is a great lady, and I'm so happy we found on another to complete this journey.
You have my heartfelt thanks. You are the best! Stacey, without you, this day could not happen.

Forever grateful,
Much love,
Sofia

Margaret, from our first phone call, before we even met, I knew I was in for something different. I asked myself, "Who is this woman, and does she really need me? Well, it turned out that you're an amazing woman with a personality to light up the sky. You produced an incredible story, and working with you is something that cannot be forgotten. From hearing about your family, your friends, and your days at work to talking about your beautiful garden, time with you has been a unique journey that I am happy to have taken. Sofia is such an amazing character; experiencing her life is something I hope many will be able to enjoy.

xoxo,
Stacey

Contents

Sofia

Dear
Maureen

Love
Margt

How It All Began

MY LIFE BECAME so repetitive, with the same thoughts racing through my head, day in and day out. When I would close my eyes, I would see a beautiful place. The colors of the flowers were bold and extraordinary. The houses were all painted beautiful pastel colors. My thoughts were so real, as if I knew this place so well. I could feel the fresh air on my face, and I could sense feelings of love, comfort, and contentment. A strange, eerie feeling would come over me, as if this were my home. Why? I would ask myself this over and over. Why do I feel like this? Why do I daydream about this place? The agonizing thoughts never seemed to end. Could there be such a place?

I had a great life and did not long for a thing. Yet hidden behind my bubbly, enthusiastic zest for life was so much fear. If you looked at me, you would never know it. There is an old cliché: you can't judge a book by its cover. That is a true fact of life—you never know what people hide behind closed doors. This place that I would see—was it real, or just a figment of my imagination? Was it that the Avellino Empire had me so overworked and overwhelmed that it just pushed me to my limits? I wanted one day to finally find out the deep secret hidden within me. So many days I would find myself sitting in Central Park, staring into the beautiful blue sky of New York City, listening to the hustle and bustle of the people around me, yet my mind was still preoccupied. I would often wonder, *Is this what happens when you reach the pinnacle of your life?*

My mind was filled and overworked with traveling to Paris, Milan, and London for Fashion Week. With endless interviews and parties, my unflagging enthusiasm kept me going. It seemed like it would never end.

I handed the airport employee my ticket. As she looked up, she said, "Good afternoon, Ms. Avellino." I just smiled. I was on a plane a few times during the month, and they were accustomed to seeing me. I really did not like to fly. For my flights, I wanted to be comfortable. I would wear jeans, a T-shirt, my mink jacket, comfortable shoes, and, of course, my Chanel bag. I sat back, had a cup of coffee, and tried to relax. When the pilot would announce the descent, I would stretch my legs out in front of me and realize I had a lot to do: visiting factories and lots of socializing. It had to be done, and I was happy to do it. It was all for business, but I wished it were for pleasure. My sisters were just as busy back in the office. Because I am the oldest child, Papa wanted me to do the traveling for the business. The truth is that I didn't have a choice; business was first. Each and every time I was on a plane, I would glance out the window and suddenly feel as though my mind was wandering off to never-never land. Then it would all begin: I would see things in the clouds.

My dear, departed, first husband, Frank, thought it was because I was overworked and my eyes were playing tricks on me. Frank even sent me to see a psychiatrist. After a few visits, the doctor told me no further treatment was necessary. All I know is that what I saw was real to me. Even as a young girl, when I would travel with my parents, I would tell them to look out the window, and I would ask them what they saw. At first they would amuse me and tell me that they saw clouds shaped like different things. However, that was not the case with me. All they saw were clouds and eventually, they just stopped paying attention to me.

It was so upsetting, and as the years went by, I never once would open the shutter that kept the sun out of the plane. I no longer wanted to see anything. Why did I see all that? What was it all about? Was I overworked, or maybe crazy?

Back in the showroom, as little girls, Papa would call, "Sofia, Isabella, Francesca! Come over here; you have to learn how to do this!" I would make a face, hesitantly reply, "Papa, I'll be right there," and slowly walk over to the steam tables. I was around nine years old. The three of us liked to play games and hide from Papa. As he would try to find us in the warehouse, we would just laugh quietly to each other. The warehouse was bright and sunny. I loved how the dust would move around in the sunlight. I would close my eyes and make believe I was in this beautiful city hidden in the clouds. I loved the wonderful world of fantasy, and then I would hear Papa yelling with his

Italian accent, "Sofia, Sofia, where are you and your sisters hiding?" I would run out, and Papa would see me and smile. Papa and I had a special connection. Maybe it was because I was the oldest—who knows?

At the time, we were on the corner of West Thirty-Fifth Street and Seventh Avenue. Papa and Mama were in the fabric business. When we were young girls, Papa had our lives designed for us. Each one of the girls would have a unique job. Papa wanted Francesca to do all the bookkeeping. She would always help him with his checking account when she was younger, so that was enough for him to see that she was good with numbers. He wanted her to handle the finances of the Avellino business. Years ago, it was a simple life. We trusted in our parents and did what they wanted us to do, no questions asked. Isabella would be in charge of all the showrooms. Therefore, when she grew up, she became the head administrator of all our showrooms. As for me, Papa would depend on me for so many things because I was the oldest. He would never give us a break; each day he taught us something new. As I look back, I guess he was correct. The Avellino Corporation became one of the biggest manufacturers in Manhattan. None of us ever complained. We had an extravagant life.

They do not make men like Papa anymore. He loved with great passion—he really loved his family. And oh, how he loved his girls. After fifty years of marriage, Papa never even looked at another woman. He would say, "Men who cheat on their family, they are weak! Like the little fish in the pond. Strong men protect their family!" Oh, how right he was.

Our family members were all hard workers, and money is something we all worked hard to obtain. Looking back, I just shook my head and wondered how we all survived. Three young Italian-American girls, struggling to make something for ourselves. The garment industry was, still is, and might always be just that: a man's world. Papa would tell us that if you learn, you will be better than any man. He taught his girls with a strong arm. Boy, was he right, and with my mother as the strength behind him, they started the business with very little.

My mother had many priceless expressions. One she would often say was, "We started with a lick and a promise." What that meant I really never knew.

The Expanding Empire

———— ◦❧◦ ————

I REMEMBER THE day so clearly when Isabella, my youngest sister, met the man of her dreams. This young, handsome, very striking, tall, blond cowboy walked into the showroom, and Isabella's jaw practically fell to the floor. It was an electric shock, as she called it. Their eyes locked, and it has been that way ever since. Isabella is a real beauty, tall with a beautiful face and smile. She has skin that most women would pay millions for and hair that cascades down her back. You will find Isabella in the gym every morning at a quarter to five. Fitness and health are very important to her, and she strives for perfection in everything she does. She has this allure to her that most men cannot resist.

Charles Nolan was his name, and he came all the way from Wyoming. He was tall, rich, handsome, and to top it off, Italian. Can you imagine finding an Italian cowboy? He had around six department stores out West and came to us to buy our line of clothes. We were no longer only in the fabric business; by then, we had a handle on every market you could think of. We all gave birth to sons, so the family got larger, and so did the business.

The summer months were almost here, and soon we would all go to the country. We loved the time in the country house; it was just so different. It was the opposite of our New York City life. The house sat on ten acres of land with the greenest grass, and to top it off, the most beautiful lake, which we had all to ourselves. When the wind blew, we would smell the trees and the flowers, and it was so refreshing. When the rain fell, it gave the air a fresh smell we loved. The country house had seventeen rooms that gave us all the space we needed. The boys really loved the freedom.

Life was wonderful, yet deep inside of me I would wonder why I so often felt like I did not belong. Why did I have those feelings? My sisters would say, "Sofia, you need to relax more and clear your mind." Sometimes, both sisters made me feel as if I were crazy; maybe I was.

The few weeks in the summer were something we all longed for just to get out of the rat race. It was a time to relax and enjoy the company of the family. During the work week, we would never even have a moment to chat. It was just work, work, and more work. The summer was our time to reflect and relax.

The ride up to the country was a smooth one. Francesca was in charge of arranging the cars and figuring out who was going with whom and at what time, when we would stop, and all the other stuff that went along with our trip. Before we got to the country house, Francesca would arrange a day out on the water with Randy, her husband.

We would all ride on Randy's four-hundred-foot Ferretti Mega Yacht. Both my mother and father loved our time on the yacht. Papa had every seagull chasing after us; feeding the birds was one of his favorite things. Francesca and Randy had been together for almost thirteen years. Her first marriage, along with her second, were long over. Francesca had one son, the very handsome, charming, intelligent, six-foot-four Jamie. He was Francesca's everything. His smile would make her melt; no matter what he wanted, he knew he could get it from his mother. Francesca was a free spirit who did everything her way. She was a striking blonde. Tall and slim, she had a flare for style and wore only the best money could buy. When she walked into a room, everyone would turn and look. Most of her clothes were bought in Milan, in Paris, or, of course, on Madison Avenue. All the clerks in the fancy shops knew her well. Both of my sisters were tall—five nine and five ten—and then you have me, standing only five foot three. I was nothing like them, and that would always drive me crazy. I looked very different from them, yet everyone would say I looked like my mother. I never saw it at all.

Francesca loved life and loved to be in love. Papa would often say she had a strong head for money and business. She knew how to invest our money and did it well. She was truly a boss at work. Not one employee would defy her words. Randy did not care that she wanted to be the boss and enjoyed the fun part of Francesca. He loved her and all that she was. He even nicknamed her "the Big Boss." He was a great guy with lots of money; he came from a wealthy family. Papa approved of him—we knew because Papa would give his head a little nod of approval for Randy. He had money, charm, and best of all, he was Italian and the ideal family man. Being married once before, Randy had a daughter, a son, and terrific grandchildren. They all adored Francesca and were very much a part of our family.

Randy's yacht was out of this world; it was so elaborate. The day was perfect, with the sun shining and the fresh, warm air. When we all arrived, the table on the deck was set for breakfast. We all knew our mother and Isabella's husband, Charles, would soon be in the galley to start preparing lunch.

Cooking was my mother's passion. The only other one who loved it as much was Charles. Together, they created unbelievable meals. We would all smell the splendid aroma coming from the galley. While they were busy preparing the food, the rest of us would sit around the yacht taking in the sun, talking, and just relaxing. The boys would lower the Jet Skis and take off alongside the yacht. Randy knew the water, having been a captain for many years; the water was his home. I would just close my eyes and daydream, but it was always the same thoughts of being on the plane and seeing all I saw out the window. I would see things, real things—whole cities with people, houses, roads, skyscrapers, and cars. Oh my God! What was wrong with me? Why in the world would I see all this? In the background, I heard everyone talking and laughing;

we couldn't have asked for better days. I would rest my head on the lounge chair and look up into the clouds, and my thoughts would become confused once again: *Who am I? Why am I here, and what is my life all about?* I was so jumbled about my life. I wanted to enjoy myself, but I was agonized with these same thoughts. My family was so tired of my talking about the same thing repeatedly. For just one day, I wanted peace.

"Sofia! Sofia!" Isabella was calling me, so off I went. My sisters and I loved to be in the sun and play like three young teenagers in the pool. In the business world, the three of us would argue daily, but outside of the office, we were as close as could be. It was the time of year that we would just relax. Throughout the day, all we did was eat, talk, and prepare for our two weeks in the summer house. The day on the water would come to an end. Randy would take the yacht to the marina, and we would once again get in the cars and continue our journey to the country house.

After the three-hour drive, seeing our grand house in the distance made us all cheerful. The house was surrounded by a huge gate with a big "A" at the top of it. As we approached the gates, they would open, and our two weeks of vacation would begin. Of course the boys would jump out of the cars first and run in different directions to check out what was going on with the property. They would make sure the pool was open and the Jet Skis were ready to go on the lake. As for the rest of us, we and the staff would gather our belongings and walk in. The house was extraordinary; there were colorful flowers in vases everywhere you looked. Both my father and mother loved gardening and couldn't wait to get out there to enjoy their flowers. Everyone was relaxed, calm, and knew that for the next two weeks, they were going to be stress-free. It was the one time of the year the Avellino family would be together and not worry about work. We ate, laughed, played cards, and sat in the sun. Sometimes we didn't even put shoes on. Often in the afternoon, I would go and relax in the library overlooking our very large garden. One day, something took me by surprise: the largest, most unusual butterfly I had ever seen. It would not leave me alone. It landed on my head, my fingers, my arm; it seemed as if it wanted me to follow it. I was startled. When it flew away, it seemed to fly higher than most butterflies and got lost in the clouds. The oddest things always seemed to happen around me.

Many nights, we would light a fire, and my parents would sit and tell us stories about the good old days. We all would be hypnotized by the roar of the flames and the intriguing stories we heard. The night would end, and one by one, we would disappear into our bedrooms.

The time flew by so quickly, and it was time to get back to the rat race.

We all knew that when we got back to work, we would miss the mornings in the kitchen with our parents. We all sat around speaking in Italian, eating hot Italian bread with butter. My mother always had so many different kinds of cheese on the table; we would sit for hours just talking to our parents. Even our boys enjoyed the early mornings. The espresso was always ready, or cappuccino, whatever anyone wanted. The mornings in the country would bring us all closer. Our parents were always sitting at the table when we woke up. My mother had her apron on, ready to make us whatever we wanted. She was her happiest when she was cooking for us.

Sometimes I would wonder what was going to happen when Papa and Mama were no longer here. When I would think of what might become of us, tears would roll down my cheeks; to imagine my family in any different way was incomprehensible. It was really just fear, and I didn't want to think about it.

My first husband died so young and left me with my three sons. The boys looked so much like their father. He was the love of my life, and after his death, I worked myself hard for many years. It was only until I met up with Tony that I even considered another man. I had many dates, but none of those men were for me. Tony had the winning combination; he would make me happy and make me smile. I could do no wrong in his eyes, and sometimes I would wonder why he loved me so damn much.

I know it was not for money. God knows, Tony was so wealthy, having been in the oil business with his father and then owning many properties in Florida. He had two sons with his wife who had passed away. In that way, we were alike, having both lost our loved ones. When I met Tony, he was always at the bar in Elaine's and had a crowd around him, as if he were a celebrity—the mayor,

or even the Godfather. He was always laughing and talking loudly and had a few ladies surrounding him, but it
did not stop him from flirting with me. He was very busy
with his crew, yet he would still glare over at me. Oddly
enough, I found that very appealing. He had a strange
allure about him that was attractive to me and absolutely
made me smile. The waiter came over and told me that
Tony wanted to pay for my lunch and buy me a drink. I
was puzzled. I looked up at the waiter and said, "Oh,
no—no thanks." The last thing I needed in my life was
a playboy. He was dressed to kill, and outside, his limo
waited for him. He seemed to be all about good times,
laughing, drinking, smoking, and what I noticed even
more was that women looked like a major part of his life.
I was not interested in that at all. However, I loved to listen to him. His voice was like no voice I had ever heard.
But my husband had died, and I did not want anything
to do with anyone. Just my boys, which was enough for
me. Sex and love were something I shut out of my life,
especially with a playboy like Tony.

Tony played eye games with me for maybe a year,
still trying to win me over. Then, one rainy afternoon in
late November, it was one of those days I wanted to stay
indoors, away from the cold dampness and just put up my
feet and watch TV. Take in an old black-and-white movie
or maybe just sit and talk on the phone—that's what I
wanted to do on days like that. Still, I went into Elaine's,
ordered my wine and salad, and there he was. Waiting for
me with a smile on his face, no entourage surrounding

him, he talked rough and very Brooklyn. It was something I was not used to because my first husband, Frank, was a well-bred Yale man. Frank had everything any woman would want until cancer took his life too early, and my Frank was gone. I missed him each and every day. He was the only one who understood my feelings and tried to help me survive all the craziness regarding what I would see and think about constantly.

Tony smiled and ordered me another glass of wine. With a smile, I thanked him. He replied, "I've been seeing you eating here for months, and you're always alone." I found it strange that he would make a comment like that. He continued to talk to me. "You are a beautiful lady. So tell me, do you have a man in your life?" I just looked at him and wanted to tell him, "It's none of your fucking business," but I did not. Rather, I replied, "You are right. I do not have a man and do not want one." I wanted to tell him that I especially didn't want one like him. Oddly enough, we both smiled and started to laugh.

He replied, "You're as fresh as you are beautiful."

No one could ever figure out my age. One thing I knew: Tony was certainly older than me!

We continued to talk through my entire lunch about my business and then about his. I found out later that he was twelve years older than me. There was something about him. He was not very tall, though he was dressed impeccably. His crisp, white shirt and fancy tie, black slacks, black cashmere blazer, and alligator loafers all added to his sexy charm. He really made me laugh for the first time in years. Seeing a wild sparkle in his eyes, something happened inside me. I felt something come alive, and I wanted him to kiss me right then and there. Instead, I simply said, "Nice to meet you, and thanks for the drink."

He stood there looking at me with pleasure in his eyes and blurted out, "You look so beautiful!"

We stood there admiring each other. He then leaned over and kissed me on my forehead. He was so sweet. He took my hand in his and said, "I hope to see a lot more of you."

With that, I walked away with a very strange sparkle in my eyes and said, "I will see you around again, I'm sure." When I walked back to my office, I was slammed with work, so I didn't have the chance to think of him again. The next morning, a package came to my office. When I opened it, I saw a keychain from Tiffany's with a very small card that said this:

> *When I was at the bar, I noticed that you*
> *needed a new keychain. I hope you like it.*
> *How about dinner next Monday at 8:00?*
> *I will pick you up. Please call me. (212)*
> *555-2009*
>
> *Thanks, Beautiful!*
> *—Tony*

I held the small card in my hand for quite a while. Maybe I needed to do something crazy; maybe that was exactly what I needed. I asked Francesca what she thought about it, and she said to go for it. I thought, *She might be right. Life is short; enjoy each day.* But a playboy in my life? That wasn't for me. I decided to not even take the box home, so it just sat at my desk. Monday came and went, and never did I call. I did not even go to my regular place anymore for lunch; I didn't need any more stress in my life. Tony did not give up. He would call me and send flowers, candy, and lunch for the staff. He chased me for months and was determined to have dinner with me, so finally I said yes.

I met him one night for dinner. He wined and dined me like I had never experienced before. The sky was the limit; I felt so comfortable in his company, as if I had known him a lifetime. He was so sweet. Even though he had a very rough, tough voice, he was a real pussycat under all that, and he was a perfect gentleman. We talked the night away; our dinner was in the Rainbow Room. When we walked in, everyone knew him. They had *his* table ready, and on the table were two dozen white roses waiting for me. Tony always had a smile on his face. When we locked eyes, something happened to us. It was like we were all alone on earth. Nothing mattered but him and me. After dinner, Tony took me to the Waldorf. We sat at the bar, talking and laughing for hours. The night was coming to an end, so we got back into the limo for him to take me home. He kissed me so tenderly that it sent chills running up my back. He paused and simply said, "How about we go to Las Vegas over the weekend?" I was startled for a second and could not comprehend the thought of going to Las Vegas with a man I hardly knew. *Boy does he move fast.* He looked into my eyes and said, "Sofia, I'm in trouble with you. You're a special lady. I want to see you again and again."

Well, I guess I was not surprised because I knew he was a player. I said to him, "Tony, that sounds like an amazing weekend. I'll call you in a day or two so I can think about it and then let you know." *A weekend in Las Vegas might be just the little break I need from life.* Tony held me in his arms. It felt so good, so warm, and so hot. I wanted him to come up with me and get in my bed. As he walked back to the limo, I thought about calling out to him to come back, but I did not.

The next morning, I called Isabella and Francesca into my office and told them all about Tony. Isabella was concerned for my safety. "Sofia, you really do not know him. You are a very rich lady, and how do you know what he's after?"

Francesca interrupted her and said, "Don't worry about Sofia and her money. She can handle anyone. You go, Sofia, and enjoy it. If you need us, remember, we are a phone call away. We have many friends in Vegas if need be." Then she added, "He sounds like a great guy to me, so just go home, forget about all the negativity, and pack!" As they walked out of my office, the phone rang, and it was Tony. He wanted that weekend with me, and I agreed to it. I arranged my work schedule and ran to tell my sisters not to tell Papa. He would be fuming with me, and the three of us just laughed. We were like three little girls, and Papa was still the boss. My sisters were thrilled for me. They said that after all those years, I needed a nice, long weekend with a man. How right they were. It had been many years since I had even kissed a man. Tony was in for a treat. I wanted to go and enjoy our weekend away. I did not even tell my boys who I was going with, just that I had a business trip, and off I went.

On the plane, we sat in first class and with a glass of wine, laughed the entire five hours away. My mind did wander, and I was afraid to open the shutter of the window. There I was with a stranger. *How am I going to tell him what I see out the window? He just wouldn't understand.* I made sure to sit in the aisle seat. Still, we kissed like teenagers, touched and loved being in each other's arms. There seemed to be some magic between Tony and me. I had never felt so good. It was long overdue for me, and maybe I was wrong about him being a playboy. I was a free woman, and I was going to enjoy my weekend.

Our hotel room looked like a bridal suite—such a fabulous room. We walked in, and as soon as the door closed, Tony grabbed me in his arms and kissed me with such passion, he knocked me right off my feet and right into the bed. Well, the truth is that we never went downstairs until late that night. We made love all day. He was a wonderful lover, so caring and so gentle. I needed him. My life was so empty for so long. His touch made me go crazy. We stayed in bed for hours, making love, talking, drinking champagne, laughing, and just enjoying each other. Finally, we wanted to go down and get something to eat and get into the casino. He kissed me all the way to the shower. As the warm water rolled over our bodies, he could not get enough of me. In this short time, I felt like I had known Tony my entire life.

I was on cloud nine. Each time he looked at me, I felt wonderful, warm, and sexy inside. It was amazing. Maybe we were just made for one another. Who knows? He was not a phony; he was the real thing. I think he fell head over heels for me, and I will say I was falling in love with him. I really couldn't wait until we got back in the room.

The next morning, my sisters called me to hear all the details, and all I could say was "Wow." They were happy for me, and we all laughed. So what was next? Was the man I met at Elaine's going to be mine? I hoped so. I was on a magic carpet ride, and I did not want it to end.

Tony and I loved each other's company. As we all know, life moves on. My husband and Tony's wife had long passed, and now we found each other. Tony and I were having the time of our lives. It was wonderful for us—traveling, shopping, eating in all the best places, and ooo, la la! The wonderful nights we shared! We went to Atlantic City for a nice, long weekend, and that's when he asked me. He held me so close to him and looked deep in my eyes. "Sofia, will you marry me?"

I almost fell off my feet. I looked at him with love in my eyes, and said "What? No ring!" That's what he loved about me. Never was I serious. We both laughed, and I screamed, "Yes, yes, yes!"

We had a very quiet wedding, with just the family—all twenty-seven of us. Mine, his, and the rest of the crew. We got married and had a wonderful dinner in one of our favorite restaurants. Tony Santa was his name, and now mine. The truth is, I was going to stay Sofia Avellino. Much too much to change. We were now Mr. and Mrs., and everyone was smiling. My boys and his boys were happy. They saw how much we loved each other, and seeing us so happy made them happy. It was great to feel connected and truly belong to someone. I loved it, and so did he.

Our honeymoon never ended. I was his sweet face, and under that rough, tough voice, he was a sweet, caring, very sexual husband who loved everything about me, and I loved him even more. We woke up in each other's arms with huge smiles. We would make love before the day began, and each night would end in love. He could not get enough of me, and I loved it! Tony and I could not be happier.

We worked hard and played even harder. We both loved the life we lived, and that was how it would stay.

The Boys

MARCELLO WAS MY youngest son. He was striking, and much taller than his brothers. He had the most beautiful green eyes; they possessed a special sparkle. Marcello had a kind and caring spirit to his personality. He loved to help others. As a young boy, in his school days, many times he would give his lunch to children that had forgotten theirs, and he would not eat. He was a good kid, and as an adult he was strong, smart, and very witty. Marcello's girlfriend was just darling. Willow was tall, very thin, and had the most beautiful red hair I ever did see. She was born in Australia and spoke so beautifully; it was like music to your ears. How they loved each other; it was so sweet to watch. Marcello was a very caring boyfriend and loved to make her happy, and it showed. Being a filmmaker, he was always traveling, and Willow did not mind. He would always bring her back a gift from the city he was in. She was his biggest fan and always had a smile on her face. Although she was not a native New Yorker, I think that's one of the things Marcello loved about her. Willow was a very talented writer, and they had so much in common. What I loved most about her is how she loved our crazy

Italian family. I began to think that one day, a wedding could be on the agenda.

Joseph, my next-oldest son, was a shining diamond in the rough. He was the best of the best. Joseph looked most like his father. He had a thin, very lean body, and he was tall and handsome with a bright smile. He had a chiseled look to his face; there was no doubt he was Italian. With his full head of hair and his sharp personality, he was someone you'd never forget. If you ever wanted to design a son, he would be the one. He did everything the right way. If we ever needed something done in the office or the house, he is the one we would call. He was Johnny-on-the-spot, as Tony would call him. He was able to build and design anything we wanted. His wife, Sabrina, was from Manhattan; she was a very rich Jewish girl. Her grandfather and my father did years of business together. She was a striking natural beauty. Her clothes were straight out of *Vogue*, and she was a very serious, confident, beautiful person. My grandsons were her life, and her schedule was completely set around their needs. The boys were the smartest in their classes and the best at everything they did. Joseph loved his family life. His home was fit for a king. When he wasn't in the office, you would always find him with a hammer in his hand, rebuilding something in his elaborate home. Sabrina couldn't be happier; she lived an extravagant life, and together they were a happy family.

My Cosmo—now, he was in a different league altogether. He had it all. He was charming, tall, and handsome, and he had a smile that could be seen a mile away, and best of all, a winning personality. Cosmo could sell you the Brooklyn Bridge. He knew how to succeed in business, and making money was his goal. He and I loved to sit and talk about everything. He had to know just what was going on in the family. He was peaceful and loved to live in harmony. Calm, cool, and handsome—that was him. Everything was beautiful in Cosmo's eyes; he loved life. His wife was Cuban, a sizzling, sexy woman. Anna had a body that could knock your eyes out and a face to match, and she loved to be in front of a stove.

Cosmo and Anna were all about life. They were the true meaning of living life large. From the day they met, they were inseparable. She was not only his lover, wife, and mother of his children, but also Cosmo's best friend. Those two, they would get in the car or plane and just take off. Their two children were beauties. They would take a tutor with them for the kids, and off they went. I could never keep up with them. They loved life, and it showed.

Isabella's boys were not married...yet. They were all playboys and dated all the top models in Manhattan. However, Richard met a lovely girl we all loved. She was from New Jersey. Richard met her in one of his restaurants, and as rumor had it, they were loving each other and having a ball. Roberto was dating a famous singer. Those boys kept us on our toes; you never knew who they were going to walk in with next. Richard was six-foot-three and had blond hair and blue eyes, like his father. Roberto was even taller, at six-foot-six; he had jet-black hair and great features. Justin, the youngest of the three, was six-foot-two and a complete combination of Isabella and Charles. He was dynamic, charming, and full of life. All three were extremely good-looking, and they knew it. Isabella's sons were her lifeline. Her boys and Charles were what she lived, laughed, and loved for.

Jamie, Francesca's son, was the family coordinator. He made sure the family was always in motion. Jamie looked like he could be the star of a soap opera with his attractive looks. He had a beautiful Greek wife, Athena. She was a doll. She was a fabulous family girl. Whenever we were all together, we could count on her to make us laugh and have a good time. She loved being around the Avellino family. She was a beautiful girl with a wonderful Greek family. They were such good people; we saw them often during the holidays. Her mother and father owned many diners, restaurants, and clubs. Like I said, Athena was a charm to the family. They had two very beautiful daughters, Paige and Arielle, whom we all loved. Every one of the boys had wonderful girls at their side, which is just the way it should be. The boys were all very close to one another and had their hands in the business constantly. By the time they were in their twenties, they were all worth millions. Papa was proud of them. No drinking, no drugs, just hard work and a good family living the good life.

Tony's boys were great. They lived in Florida and were very close to him. They all did very well. Tony and I would jump on and off planes to make sure that they were always a part of our lives. That is how it was, and that is how we liked it. As some people say, "It worked for us."

The Party

————— ✦ —————

THE DAY WAS very busy for us girls. Isabella and Charles were going to celebrate their twenty-fifth wedding anniversary. Charles was giving her a big party in the Rainbow Room. The day started out with dark clouds and rain. My mother said that meant more good luck for the happy couple. None of us wanted to hear rain, even if that meant good luck. It was really just a big mess, but we all made the best of it.

We all spent that morning together in our favorite hair salon on the corner of Sixty-Ninth Street and Madison Avenue. We had been going there for years. With all the rain, the salon was empty. Our mother went first; she had to run back home right after because we had guests coming in from all over the place. My mother's youngest brother, Uncle Salvatore, and his wife, Aunt Jill, were in from Dallas and staying at The Waldorf. My mother catered to her family and was hurrying so she could make her brother his favorite lunch—eggplant parmesan.

We had a car waiting out front so none of us would get wet. We all sat in the salon talking and laughing all morning. Our daughters-in-law were with us. All three of them were all close with me. Not a day would go by that they did not check in to see how I was doing. My Anna had a warm and sensitive charm to her and she and I became friends when it all began with her and Cosmo. She was full of life and loved to laugh. She would sometimes call me three or four times a day to keep me up to date. My grandson, Mikey, and granddaughter, Dee, would go up to the office when they were on their way to their fencing classes. They just loved to go up to the showrooms and look around.

Sabrina was always on the run. Many days, she would stop at the office with the boys between their ball games. The kids would run into my office and give me a kiss. They loved running around saying hello to everyone up there, and I loved having them. Sabrina and I would sit, have a cup of coffee, and enjoy a nice chat. She would show me all the wonderful things my son was doing in their new home. She often would stop by with her mom. Through the years, her mother and I had become good friends. Sabrina was a good person and came from a wonderful, good family.

My Laura was always pleasant and never had a bad word to say about anyone. It was great spending time in Florida with her. Then I had Willow. Not a daughter-in-law yet, but one day, hopefully soon, I hoped it will happen and that she would become an Avellino. She was a sweet-heart. Like I said, all my girls were just fabulous. Francesca's daughter-in-law, the Greek goddess, was also a pleasure to be around. She loved our family, and Francesca was always very involved with her granddaughters. The girls loved to go shopping with their Grandmamma. Those two were the best-dressed little girls around. Being a mother-in-law is never easy, but I thank God we had a great family and life was always fantastic.

We all did things together and had a good time doing them. Francesca's granddaughters, Paige and Arielle, and my granddaughter, Deanna, all got along well. All the grandkids were beautiful, talented children. I guess all grandparents feel the same way, and that is how it should be. Deanna was something special. She loved to sit and talk with me. She had a talent for photography; it was amazing. The thing that interested me most was the way she talked about mermaids. She was convinced that in another life, she was a beautiful mermaid. Her boy-friend went out and bought her a mermaid tail, and she would use it in the pool. Surprisingly, she really looked like a mermaid.

All the grandkids kept us on our toes. Michael, Nicholas, and Dominick were great boys. Nick and Dom were always engaged in some sort of ball game. They both had the most adorable, funny personalities. Michael was the affectionate one and was forever gathering information on and learning about World War II. He knew more about it than most adults. Paige and Arielle were our dancers and in competitions all over the place. Then we had our Florida girls. They were stunning and sur-rounded themselves with fashion. It was overwhelming to see all the kids. Life is so precious, so we should never take anything for granted. All the children had many talents, but Deanna intrigued me simply because she felt like she was something else. God knows, her Nana shared the same thoughts.

Fortunately, I had a loving family and amazing friends. To some of them, I had the ability to express my feelings. So along with my wonderful husband, you might say, I had it all. We laughed and talked all morning. Isabella was the funniest of the three sisters. My father always said she belonged on the stage. She had the talent to entertain people, and she did it very well. We talked about marriage and how lucky she was to have her Charles. He planned the party all by himself. I was very sure the party would be a smashing success. Everything he did, he did well.

I decided I needed an extra cup of coffee for the morning, so I went across the street to get coffee for everyone. When I walked back into the salon, I was standing in the doorway, and Isabella and Francesca had their backs to me and were talking. I heard my name mentioned, and though I didn't want to listen to what they were saying, I stood there quietly. We never hid things from one another, but I heard Isabella say to Francesca, "I'm very worried about Sofia, Francesca. What do you think? Lately she is just so preoccupied with everything; she is just not herself."

Francesca replied "maybe she is just overworked. After all, this is our busiest season."

Isabella added, "It torments me because Sofia constantly says she's seeing things that we don't and that she's not like us at all." I stood very still. I was upset that they were worried about me. I wondered, *What is happening to this family? Am I really that odd?* I would have prayed to the Blessed Mother daily if she could help me find what my strange feelings were all about. Sometimes I would lose my faith because she would never answer me. Was I going to always upset the entire family? Just then, both the girls stood up and greeted me by the door. The day went on, and I never discussed what I heard.

It was around seven o'clock when we all left for the Rainbow Room. The party was a big event, and anyone who was anyone in the garment business was present. Isabella looked like she stepped out of a *Glamour* magazine and looked fabulous. The party was like a fantasy: music, food, and beautiful people. The room was decorated for royalty. Charles made a toast to his beautiful wife and handed her a box. All we heard was, "Oh my God! Oh my God!" In her hands was a beautiful six-carat diamond ring. Oh my good God, when I saw the ring, it was the most beautiful piece of jewelry I had ever seen. Charles walked Isabella to the dance floor, and they moved around like they were on a cloud. As they glanced into each others eyes, it was enchanting to watch. Charles certainly knew how to give a party. The whole night didn't miss a beat; the party was a big extravaganza and a huge success.

Bravo to Charles.

Friends

❧ ❧

ONCE A MONTH, I got together with my girlfriends and this time we were going to start the day at Salina's. She had lived in the city for most of her life. Her husband had one of the most successful real estate businesses in the city. Her children were her life, and she was all about family. Her view of life was so uncannily positive, and she truly believed in good and bad energy. She always had a helping hand, no matter what. You would find her all over the place, helping the entire human population. Salina and her husband were a fabulous couple. Her daughter did cosmetic dentistry for the stars. Salina was also blessed with twin boys. One of them was an opera singer with the most magnificent voice. Many nights we went to see him perform in the Metropolitan Opera House. His twin brother was a successful attorney. Salina was tall and striking, with very straight, long, black hair. She had a wonderfully hysterical personality and made us laugh when we wanted to cry. It felt good to be silly, and she had the talent to make us laugh.

Carm was on her way to meet us ladies. She owned many restaurants in Manhattan, so she was constantly busy. She and her husband had four daughters, and all of them had their own Italian restaurants. She had all the right ingredients and all the answers for us ladies. Carm loved to look her best and spent hours getting ready for our get-togethers because most of her days were spent in a white apron in the restaurant. She kept her hair very short, and she always had on fabulous jewelry and a hat. If I had to describe her in one word, I would say "happy." She was always traveling back and forth to Italy. The combination of us girls was perfect. We all loved one another for who we were, and we had a lifetime of memories to talk about.

Lillianna and Marco were in from Sicily; Lillianna was a treasured person in my life. She had a heart as big as Rome itself; it always felt good to be around her. Lilly was a light-skinned blonde with long legs, a sexy frame, and huge breasts. Her husband's eyes never left her. He was madly in love with her, and it was warm and wonderful to watch. They were a smooth Italian team. Her husband made millions in diamonds because his father left him diamond mines in Africa. They didn't have a care in the world. In Italy, they lived in luxury. They had three sons who were all successful. Their youngest son, Carmine, was a high-ranking model in Manhattan. He often would stop in to see me. He was so much like his mother, with a broad smile and the eyes of a saint—the bluest eyes you can imagine. Their oldest son, Mario, and his wife, Maria, lived on Long Island and had built a fabulous business; both of them were interior decorators. Lilly's middle son,

Giovanni, was single and produced TV reality shows. He had a lineup of girlfriends a mile long; he was an Italian Adonis. Lilliana's one brother, Giuseppe, and his wife, Teresa, both worked in the mayor's office and had a beautiful apartment in the city. Lilly was in for a few months. She and her husband loved Manhattan and had to get a dose of it once a year. I truly missed her throughout the year. Our meetings with the girls were just not the same when she was not around. She and Marco had a penthouse that they kept for when they were in town, which is where we would have our lunches. Sometimes all four of us would talk at once, just like teenagers. It was as if we were the real "Sex in the City" girls. We truly had a connection as we journeyed through the scheme of life. We enjoyed each day.

My friend, Marcy, was in town, but she was not able to join us. We didn't get to see her very often, simply because she was a very successful publicist who was always involved with a movie, book, or publication. However, we would have long talks on the telephone, and sometimes I would use her as my therapist—especially when I had those sleepless nights. She would tell me I had too much stress with my daily life and had to calm down. Marcy was bright and witty all rolled into one. She had a very soothing voice, and it was a pleasure talking to her when I needed that shoulder to lean on. When she was around, we did manage to jump in to Bloomingdale's and have a quick lunch. Marcy and her husband would occasionally join Tony and me for drinks and dinner in the city.

Traveling so much, you get to see the same people on the planes. Much to my surprise, I met a beautiful older woman, Marietta, one day. She was full of life at eighty-three years old, and still loved to shop on the Champs Elysées. She always looked like she came right out of Saks. She and I would always chat as we traveled back and forth from New York to Paris. She lived in Manhattan, and she and I would often meet for coffee. She was a pleasure to be around and helped me to get through the flights that I dreaded so much.

As we all got older, life looked different. It was only Lilly who knew I was troubled and wanted to find some peace, to finally learn about me, Sofia Avellino. Tony and I would go off to Sicily on quick business trips. I would call Lilly to meet for lunch, and we would walk the streets of Sicily in the October sunshine. As much as we would talk and talk, we would never find the answer to my deep secret. As we would sit with cappuccino, I would pour my heart out to her and keep repeating, "Lilly, I feel like I'm losing my mind." Her compassionate personality would come out and tell me everything was OK. I thanked her for being such a great friend, but I could see in her eyes that she felt concerned and worried.

It always helped me seeing all the girls. We would shop, laugh, talk, make fun of ourselves, and enjoy our day, like four schoolgirls without a care in the world. The best times are always with good friends.

Every time Tony and I would run off to Florida, we would be sure to go see all our friends who lived there.

However, our favorite place to stop was the beautiful Pompano Beach. Tony and I had a wonderful penthouse apartment on the ocean. No surprise to us, there were a few TV stars in our building. Our friends, Shirley and Morris, had been in the building for more than twenty years and loved it. We always had a great time with them by the pool. I loved being in Florida and sitting on our terrace, staring into the ocean. I would think maybe out there I would find some answers. The sound of the ocean and the warm breeze made me feel so comfortable inside. I was constantly searching for answers. In the darkness, I would sit and worry about what I had to face one day. I knew in my heart that something was coming, but what, I couldn't even begin to imagine.

Back in New York, Gigi and I had been friends since we were twelve years old. We could not be more opposite and still were the best of friends. Even our mothers knew one another. Gigi's mother was a very famous children's-book author, and her father was a famous opera singer. She lived in the Hamptons in a huge mansion on the beach. We saw each other very little but had still managed to talk on the phone each day for the past forty-five years. Money was not an issue in her lifestyle. Her family had dabbled in the market and made millions, so she was set. You would not think it by looking at her; she was very beautiful, yet very plain. Quiet, sweet, and naïve, she was different from me, and our ways of thinking were different. Gigi was very good-looking and so intelligent, a Yale graduate. Her first husband, Al, was her complete opposite, they came from two different worlds. Gigi loved him more than life itself. Al was a Vietnam veteran and loved the lifestyle he had with Gigi. They were graced with two beautiful children and had a family life better than most people can ask for. Sadly, one day it came to a halt when Al suddenly had a massive heart attack and passed away. As time went on, Gigi met a wonderful older man who adored her. His name was Phillip, and he was a nice blend: tall and good-looking. He was from Vermont and lived in a beautiful castle there. She met him while on vacation there. Gigi's daughter worked for the FBI, and her son had his own chain of stores. Forty-five years of friendship is quite a relationship. All of us had good lives; we were all truly blessed. Raising our children was a great experience. We both had busy lives but managed to enjoy the early years with the kids.

I was blessed to have so many wonderful people in my life. My mother always taught us to be warm and welcoming to all. As for me, my circle was deep. My friends were not around me all the time, simply because my life and theirs did not allow it. Sandy moved out to New Jersey. She was a wonderful, carefree, funny woman whom I had known since I was twelve years old. She and I would meet up occasionally and run off to Atlantic City. Then I had my girlfriend, Susie V. Now, she was Mother Teresa in disguise. We could go for months without hearing from one another and then just pick up the phone and talk as if no time had gone by.

My Brooklyn girl, Marie, and the Gio family were the best around. We were all hard workers and kept our friendship all these years. Last but not least, Lorraine and her wonderful family held a special place in my heart. One of her best qualities was that she could understand me, and I could understand her.

As we wander through the journey called life, it's sensational to have so many people whom you can count on. I thank God for my friends and my family. I often wonder what they all would think of me if they knew the real Sofia. So many days, I was tempted to tell everyone and never had the nerve to speak up. Just Lily had some idea of what I felt and lived with. That is only because one time in Italy, I was so frazzled while sitting in the Piazza having lunch, and there it was—the same white horse with the same lady I had seen in Manhattan. How could it have been?

Family Night Out

─── ⚜ ───

WE WERE PLANNING a night out with the family—that meant all the cousins, aunts, and uncles were going to come. We called our event planner, Crystal. She was a friend of mine and was always ready to plan a party for us. I told her what I wanted, and she said she would get it all done. Usually we would pick a place, and she would go there and place the orders, decorate for us, and it would be a fun night out with the family.

Uncle Salvatore and Aunt Jill were coming in from Dallas. They were world travelers, so as long as they were not going to be somewhere else in the world, they would be here. It was easy for them to travel; they could hop on and off the planes each week because their son was a pilot. Their daughter was an attorney and would fly in with her two girls. Their other son was coming in to join us from Denver and was bringing his whole family.

Through the years, I had become the head of the family and would always arrange the events. I loved keeping us all together. I would set up the event and then put it in Crystal's hands. She worked for us a few times a year. She was such a happy person, and I loved spending time with her. We would often go out for coffee. Her very posh office was in the city, and she would come running over to see me every once in a while.

My cousins would come in from everywhere, trying their best not to miss a night out with all of us. My cousin, Charlotte, and I could sit, laugh, and get silly over anything. It had been that way since we were little children. Sometimes, when we were together, we would look through old photo albums, and there we were, stuck together like glue. Strangely enough, here we were, forty years later and still as close as could be. Charlotte was very religious and went to church daily. She tried to take me along, but my busy schedule didn't allow me the time. She believed I would find peace of mind if I would go to church more often. I took her advice a few times and found that sitting in church was tranquil and beautiful, and I would find peace. While sitting in the pew, I felt comfortable and relaxed. Being close to God was helpful. But as soon as the doors swung open and the sunshine glared in my face, it snapped me back to reality, and I would once again be the mixed-up, crazy lady, Sofia. Charlotte would tell me, "Sofia, you have a life like a fairytale; you should be so happy. A man who adores you, beautiful children and grandchildren, a thriving business. A life that some people don't even get a taste of." Even with all that, I still had the feeling of not fitting in.

Charlotte's sister, Amanda, and her husband, Thomas, were living in Boston. Whenever Amanda would come in to the city, she, Charlotte, and I would often get lunch and do some shopping. It was always a fun afternoon. Amanda's husband was an avid golfer. Every time he was golfing in Myrtle Beach, Tony and I would try to join him. The Italians sure know how to keep family near. My mother had three sisters and four brothers; the only surviving sibling was Salvatore. All the cousins stayed in touch with each other. My cousin, Jonathan, was like the brother I never had. He was a contractor, and any time we called him, he would come right over to help. Jonathan's two brothers lived in Colorado, and we visited them at their ski lodge when we could. One of his brothers was a famous photographer for a well-known wild-life magazine. Larissa, the talented singer in our family, was always in charge of entertainment.

All my cousins were there. We always had a great time; everyone showed up dressed to kill, in tuxedos and evening gowns. The limos would pull up, and we all had the biggest smiles on. But I was still so preoccupied with my thoughts from the flight I had been on only hours earlier.

I rushed into the restaurant and realized I had forgotten my purse in the limo. The ordeal on the plane had been very frightening, more so than ever before. The images in the clouds were just so detailed and more realistic than they had ever been. I couldn't get them out of my mind. When I got back to the limo to grab my purse, I looked up and saw a beautiful white horse staring at me. It startled me even more than I already was. The person riding the horse was, surprisingly enough, a beautiful young woman who would not stop staring at me. It felt so weird that when I looked at her, it was as if I knew her.

That made me run back into the restaurant. There was just something about what had just happened that sent chills running through my body. I knew I had to face everyone in a few minutes, so I went into the ladies' room to calm myself down. I realized how blessed I was to have all my family there that night.

Aunt Rosa's daughter and son-in-law, Marcelina and Bruce, owned one of the biggest scuba-diving schools and shops in the Hamptons, where they lived. They both spent more time in the water than they did on land. Their future plan was to move to St. Thomas. Even at seventy, Aunt Rosa looked amazing. She was a very popular decorator who designed half of Manhattan. She loved us girls, and of course all her nieces and nephews, and we all loved her just the same. Everything turned out great and looked fabulous. Hearing our cousin, Larissa entertain us all was a highlight of the evening. We all sat, ate, and laughed all night; it was something we did once or twice a year. It was a great night out with everyone. Larissa's brother, Franco, and his wife, Connie, also lived in the city in a very luxurious brownstone. When Franco wasn't working as meteorologist, he was behind the stove. On many occasions, I'd turn on the news and hear him giving the latest weather updates. Connie had the most beautiful garden in the middle of the city.

Life was good, and it was clear that we had a good family and loved one another.

At the end of the night, Isabella, Francesca, and I would kick off our shoes and sit and talk. All the boys with their families had left, as well as the grandchildren—Nicholas, Dominick, Paige, Arielle, Deanna, and Mikey. Our Florida family couldn't make it, so we missed seeing our beautiful Nicolette and Jacqueline; however, they were going to be in the next day. We finally had some peace and quiet. It really got hectic with all six of the grandkids—my four and Francesca's two. We loved them and loved to be around them, but when they left, oh, the wonderful peace and quiet.

When I got home that night and tried to go to sleep, my eyes just wouldn't stay shut. I tossed and turned for hours. Thank God, Tony had had a few drinks and was sound asleep. Thinking about that strange event outside kept me up and so puzzled. When I finally managed to fall asleep, I had bizarre dreams. I dreamed of a lady standing in a garden, claiming to be my mother. I started to ask her questions about my life, and as soon as she opened her mouth to answer, I woke up. I can't help but wondering what caused those dreams. Was it the great party and seeing all the family? Or was it the strange feeling I got when I saw the woman on the white horse? I closed my eyes, and tears rolled down my cheeks. For the first time in many, many years, I was truly scared.

The following evening, Tony and I were so excited, we were going to spend time with his two boys and their families at the Ritz-Carlton. They had made dinner reservations and planned a fabulous evening for all of us. Tony's granddaughters were stunning. Fashion was everything to them. I really loved them, and they enjoyed spending time with Tony and me. We would always talk about shopping, eating, and going back to Florida to see them. I often wondered if Tony said anything to them about my strange thoughts. I kept it from them simply because I didn't want them think I was a nut. I wanted them to know their father was in good hands and well taken care of.

All about Papa

PAPA WAS GROWING more frail with each passing day. He no longer was able to stay in the office for a whole work day. I would see his eyes grow tired right after lunch. I would say to him, "Papa, *andare a casa*." He would nod his head yes and say, "In a few minutes, I will relax."

I loved it when he spoke in Italian. The entire family wrote, spoke, and read Italian. Papa and Mama made sure of that. The boys would show off from time to time and would talk to Papa only in Italian. My mother was not really one to fool around; she was a very serious woman. She would stay in the background and observe, listening to everyone. Our parents lived in a huge Manhattan apartment facing Central Park. It had all the Old World charm that only our mother could create. In her younger days, the business was her life. As she aged, she left it to us girls and all the grandsons. Papa was still running the show, and she knew that. She would stay busy with planning our meals.

Every weekend, it was a commitment that we all had dinner together. It would be a day to relax and just let our hair down. We would talk around the dinner table for hours. Our mother was such a fabulous cook. Papa had a full-time staff for Mother; nevertheless, she still liked doing all the housework and cleaning on her own. She insisted that no one could cook or clean the way she did. In a way, she was right. Their apartment was like something out of a magazine. Our mother had a flair for decorating.

After we ate a seven-course meal that was out of this world, Isabella, Francesca, and I would go for a walk. We needed to move around after eating so much, and all our boys would follow. Jamie and Joseph would walk and talk about all their new adventures; they were always starting something new. Cosmo and Justin loved to walk with Papa. They would walk and talk, speaking in Italian, and you could hear them laughing a mile away. Richard and Roberto were enjoying their conversation, talking about the new motorcycles they were about to buy. The family was always on the move. We would wander in the park like it was our own backyard. While we were walking, my mother had the staff cleaning and getting dessert ready.

Coffee and cake is a big event in any Italian home. Let's face it—food is a big event. Everything important happens over a good meal. Isabella, Francesca, and I would walk and talk about what we had to do during the week. Each one of us had our own unique job in the company, and we all did it well. After work on Mondays, we would sometimes plan to go shopping.

From a distance, we heard Joseph calling, "Let's go back. Dessert is ready!" It was funny how our parents were very much in charge of all of us. It was beautiful and wonderful all rolled into one. You might say we had the perfect family.

You would never think that Papa was approaching his ninetieth birthday next February. He had a nice head of hair, was never overweight, and took good care of himself. Although he did have a love for junk food, he ate it in moderation. That was the key to his longevity; he would never overdo anything. Our parents were simple.

Our mother was a simple lady. No one would take her for one of the richest women in Manhattan. She loved to cook, clean, and enjoy her family. She would enjoy the simple things life had to offer. Life was grand for my mother; her wealth and love made it seem to be the perfect life.

The boys were always around Papa. He really loved his grandsons, all seven of them. He made sure they would have lives made rich by a successful business. Their futures were secure the moment they were born. The Avellino family would live on because Papa would make sure they all worked hard.

Now that the boys were older, they all had their own place in the family business. My nephews, Jamie and Richard, decided they would venture out and start something new. They opened a fabulous restaurant on the Lower East Side. Even though they had a few high-end restaurants, they still had a lot going on in the Avellino industry. They were powerful salesmen and were very successful. Roberto was very dedicated to our company and knew the business in and out. Roberto was Isabella's son, and they were both involved with all the showrooms and publicity. Joseph and Cosmo were very successful salesmen. They sold our merchandise everywhere in the United States and began taking us international.

Now, my son, Marcello, our movie maker, didn't work with us all that much. Papa did not mind because he loved watching all the short films Marcello made. Marcello was different from Cosmo and Joseph—different in the same way that I was different from Francesca and Isabella. This would often make me wonder if he had the same crazy thoughts I had, but I could never gather the courage to approach him about it. His passion for the film industry was uncanny. He lived for that one break to see his name in lights, and I knew that one day he would make it. He has been involved in film since he was able to talk. Our boys were all successful.

Last but not least, our Justin, the King of the Road, was still in school and could do no wrong in Papa's eyes. He did very little in the Avellino Corporation. He came in after school and sat with me in my office. We would talk about his latest flame, who happened to be a beautiful model named Ali. She was tall and gorgeous. I think the two of them were the perfect team. This was Justin's last year of high school. He was in Stuyvesant, and the next step was Columbia University. For his graduation, he couldn't wait to get his new Corvette. The biggest fight he and Ali would have was over the color. He really didn't want to leave the city and all his family, and he certainly did not want to leave his girlfriend, Ali.

Justin had a very caring nature and would get involved with each and every charity. Helping the poor, helping the sick, he was always in front of the major hospitals raising money. All our boys were growing into men. All were very wealthy, good-looking men. Nevertheless, Papa had a sadness in his eyes. When I caught him off-guard, I would sometimes see him looking out into the empire he built for us. I knew he didn't want to leave us, but it's something we all end up thinking about.

My mother was home; she was not feeling up to par anymore. We were soon going to lose our parents. It was hard to comprehend life without them. I was always the strongest because I knew Papa depended on me to keep us all together. But why me? I was always searching for answers, about the secret to my life. It was a fear I had to live with, a fear that I was the different daughter.

I was up very early one morning to take Papa to the doctor. I called down to the doorman to have my car waiting out front. As I put on my coat, Tony came up behind me. Even in the early morning, he would tell me how beautiful I was. "With the sunlight shining on your face, you look like an angel, my angel."

Before we left for the doctor's appointment, Tony said he wanted to come back home afterward and have a hangout day because he missed me. As he put his arms around me, he said, "Come on, Sofia, I miss you." I had to explain to him that my father was not feeling well, and taking care of him was my priority. I wanted him to go home and rest for a few days. If I told Papa I was not going into the office, he would be fuming, and I did not want to upset him. I told Tony, "Maybe one day this week I will stay home, and you and I can play." I gave him a kiss and ran to the door. As I put my hand on the doorknob, he said, "Sofia, I love you. Good luck at the doctor."

Tony was really a wonderful man, and all he wanted was to make me happy. He did anything and everything for me, and I did the same for him. For some reason, I was always confused and never as happy as I wanted to be.

That day, my focus had to be on Papa. The weather was cold. It looked like snow. Everyone was rushing around in the city. I asked the concierge at the desk to call my parents' building and tell my father to be downstairs and that I would get there in just a few minutes. We all lived within a few blocks of each other, so it would take no time at all. I saw Papa standing out there, up against the wall as if the wall were holding him up. I asked Sal, my driver, to go out and get Papa. I watched Sal as he approached my father. Papa looked like he was in pain and seemed very happy to see Sal because Papa really needed someone to hold onto. He got in the car, looked at me, and didn't say a word. He put his hand on mine, and when I looked up at him, it looked like he wanted to cry. In Italian, I would talk to Papa and ask what was wrong and why he wasn't feeling well. His legs were very bad; they just didn't want to move anymore. We were hoping the doctor would be able to help him and find out what was wrong.

It was only nine in the morning. I was an early bird; that's why Papa would like to do things with me early. I was on time, never late. Sal helped Papa out of the car. I nodded at him to walk him to the doctor. I thought we might need a wheelchair for Papa, and as I went to get it, Papa nearly took my head off, shouting, "I am not dying! I will not have you push me around! Never!" I was thinking it would be easier for him but quickly dropped the idea.

The doctor popped his head into the waiting room, which was empty. The doctor greeted us and told us he'd be with us shortly. A minute later, the nurse called us in and checked Papa's blood pressure, and like always, it was too high. The doctor came in and said, "Cosmo, what can I do for you today?" Dr. Levin had been our doctor for more than twenty years. Papa started to talk to him in Italian. I quickly had to tell him, "English, Papa." Papa then asked me to explain to Dr. Levin how he was feeling, that his legs were very heavy and didn't want to move like they used to. The doctor asked me to leave the room while he examined him.

About thirty minutes later, he called me back in. "Sofia, the only thing I can suggest is to bring your father over to the rehabilitation center on Twenty-Third Street." It was a nursing home; however, on the third floor, they had a rehab center where they could help with Papa's mobility. I saw nothing wrong with his legs, but I thought maybe therapy would help him. They recommended that he stay there for five to six weeks. I didn't understand why Papa had to stay there. Why couldn't he just go home at night? Dr. Levin said that the therapy would work better if Papa spent the time there. He said that if there was improvement within two weeks, Papa could go home. We would have to talk about it. Dr. Levin said that rest would do him good. Papa had never been away from my mother; for that matter, he had not been away from any of us.

I told Dr. Levin that I would have to talk about it with my sisters and my mother before we made a decision.

He asked, "What about you, Cosmo? What do you say?"

Papa responded, "Well, if it will help me, I will go." In Italian, I said to Papa that we would talk about it at home. The doctor got up from behind his desk, put down his glasses, and gave me a kiss good-bye. He saw that I had great concern in my eyes.

"Sofia, it will do him good. Your father needs to rest. You can go over to see him any time. Try it, and if after a few days he does not like it, he can go home."

I looked very puzzled. Anyway, I thanked Dr. Levin for his time, he gave my father a handshake, and out we went.

Sal stopped at my father's apartment. Papa gave me an argument about staying home that day. I said, "Papa, please just go up and relax. We will take care of business today. We had the best teacher money can buy— you. Just relax today. After work, we will come over to talk about your stay at Saint Mary's. OK, Papa? Talk to you when I get to the office."

He turned to me and thanked me for being a good girl. We both smiled, and Papa disappeared in the building. I took a deep breath and started to cry. My thoughts about leaving him in a nursing home were not promising. I had no faith in that institution at all.

After work, we all went up to talk to my parents and knew we would have to make a decision. It was unanimous: we were going to try. Papa wanted to get better, and he thought a stay at the rehab center would help.

The next morning, Jamie, Joseph, Isabella, and I took him over to the nursing home. As we entered, the smell of the place made me sick, but I said not a word. My sisters and I thought it might help him. Isabella and I went up to make sure that Papa was all settled. We left the boys there to make sure he was in good hands. Isabella and I bent over to kiss Papa good-bye. He had tears in his eyes, and we were both very surprised to see that. "Papa, what is wrong?" I asked. "If you do not want to stay here, we will take you home."

"No," he replied.

It's sad to think your life is coming to an end. He looked up at both of us and said, "Girls, enjoy your lives. Time goes so fast, and one day you will have to say good-bye." He looked like a sad puppy. As Isabella and I walked down the long hallway, we were both silent in our own thoughts. The words Papa had just spoken tugged at our hearts.

Papa hated his stay at St. Mary's. We all went back and forth each day for two weeks. The treatment did not seem to be helping him at all. My mother was unable to get there each day; she was not feeling well herself. The boys would go up to see their grandfather. As soon as they left his room, they would call us, yelling, "We have to get Grandpa out of this place!"

Papa had been given too many medications, and they were not working well. He was just not himself; the strong businessman we all knew was gone.

One afternoon, I went and took him home. He had a nurse day and night, and a physical therapist came to the house two times a week. Papa did a lot of sleeping. He was not even interested in the business anymore; he just wanted to be left alone. He ate and went back to sleep. We would go up each day to the house to see him, but he was not the same man he used to be. My mother would sit by his bed and read to him. He did not want to watch TV or listen to the radio. His friends would call to go visit him, but he did not want them there. We did it his way; we were all so uptight. We were waiting for the day when the nurse would call us to get to his house.

It was spring again. The flowers were blooming, and the air was warm and fresh. For Easter Sunday, we were all going to be at our parents' house. Charles would cook along with my mother; she wanted us all there for the holiday. We were at the office and were all going home early on Good Friday. That was never a work day, but that week, we were so upset about Papa that keeping busy at work was the best thing for all of us.

That morning, at about 3:30 a.m., my phone rang. I answered, and it was my father's nurse. She said that Papa's blood pressure was too low, and she wanted to take him to the hospital. She had already called 911 and was now just waiting for the ambulance to take him to New York University Hospital. I sat down and started to cry. I knew this was it; Papa was leaving us. I called the girls, and we all left to get to the hospital. When we entered Papa's hospital room, he wasn't breathing right. We could see he wasn't doing well. The thought of him leaving us made my eyes fill with tears. As they rolled down my face, he opened his eyes. He knew his girls were there, and he wanted us to stand close to him. He wanted to tell us something, so we walked closer to him. He tried to speak, but no words could come out. We all sat with him for hours. The doctor came in and told us he didn't have much longer. We knew we would all stay and just talk with each other and remember all our days with Papa, telling stories and laughing. In a strange way, I think Papa was listening to us. He had a happy smirk on his face and would move every so often. Francesca went to get us coffee. It was almost midnight when his doctor came back one more time and told us to go home. But we were not leaving, and that was definite. We walked over to the bed, and in our own way, we said good-bye to Cosmo Joseph Avellino. It was Holy Saturday, the day before Easter. The nurse came, and then two more, and then another. They asked us to leave, and we all started crying hysterically. Isabella, Francesca, and I were losing our best friend, our lifeline, our father.

When the nurse and everyone walked out of the room, they told us to go back and say our final good-byes. My sisters and I walked into the room and surrounded the bed. One by one, all seven of the boys walked in behind us. Jamie walked over and leaned over Grandpa. He cried and said, "Come on! This cannot be. You can't leave us. We need you, Grandpa." He fell into his mother's arms, and they were both crying hysterically.

Isabella leaned over Papa and touched his face. She fell on to his chest and said, "It's me, Papa, your baby."

We were all hysterical. Justin walked over and said, "Please Grandpa, can't you get better?"

Papa moved and looked up at all of us. Tears were falling down his face. My mother sat in a chair with her head in her hands. Roberto was comforting her. She then walked over to the bed and spoke so quietly to him, like she was telling him a secret. All we could hear was, "Cosmo, don't worry. The girls and grandchildren will take care of me and the business." Everyone else left the room, and Francesca, Isabella, and I were left standing there like we were in a bad dream. For a split second, Papa opened his eyes, looked up at all three of us, and whispered softly, "I love you, my girls."

That was it—our Papa was speaking his last words, taking his last breath. This was the worst night of our lives. It was hard to believe that he was gone. It was a very strange feeling. How could this be? No way! I could not believe it. It was a nightmare that I needed to wake up from, but no, it was the truth. It was over. That night, as we all walked out of the hospital, our lives were changed forever. Cosmo Avellino was gone. The next day was Easter Sunday, the holiest and happiest day for Roman Catholics.

For us, it was the day of mourning. It was not the wonderful, joyous Easter we were all used to. We sat around the table, and for most of the day, we were just talking and crying and preparing for the wake.

Papa's instructions were that he wanted his wake to last for only one day. So we would follow his wish, and it would be only one day. The wake was like a whirlwind to us. People were everywhere—inside, outside, down the block. The boys and our other family members were there all day and all night. We knew the next day would be the most difficult. That night, we all went home to try and sleep. We were all up at dawn; we had to be at the funeral parlor at eight. As we gathered around Papa, we were all crying and not sure how to handle ourselves. One by one, we said our good-byes. Isabella, Francesca, and I could not believe what we were about to face, a new world without our father. The heartbreak of losing him is unbearable.

The day of the funeral, we all got out of the limousines, and with heavy hearts, we all held hands and walked behind the coffin of the late Cosmo Avellino. We climbed the stairs, and the church doors opened. The priest greeted us; he knew us well. He smiled at Mama and gave her a warm and caring hug. With great care and concern, he said, "Frances, we will miss him at mass, and I will miss him as a dear friend."

My sisters and I walked in behind Mama. He smiled when he saw us girls. "The Earth is losing a wonderful man," he said. "Your Papa will do wonders up there in

heaven." The church was full of people—business associ-
ates, workers, store merchants, family members. Everyone
came to say farewell to our father. Monsignor Gallo got up
and said so many beautiful words about Papa, recounting
all his years of service to the community, his devotion to
his family, and how he was part of the garment industry
for more than sixty years. He even told a few jokes about
Papa and made everyone smile. My mother, sisters, and
I were all dressed in black from head to toe and had big,
beautiful hats with black veils over our faces so no one
could see the hurt and the tears that were in our eyes.
The mass was beautiful and filled with wonderful church
hymns. My son, Marcello, did the eulogy. He spoke beautifully and told great stories about his grandfather. Then
Justin spoke. He stood there with tears running down his
face, and his words made us all cry. As the mass came to
an end, we gathered our belongings and headed out to
take Papa to his final resting place.

We had a police escort because we wanted to pass
the office building. Manhattan was so busy during the day,
there was no way we could do it without the police. Papa
had a beautiful funeral; the hearse was followed by ten
limousines and a beautiful flower car. The ceremony at the
gravesite was unbelievable. My father had a twenty-one-
gun salute. Seven soldiers stood next to the coffin, and
each shot three rounds. Papa was a World War II veteran
and loved the military. At the end of the ceremony, they
folded up the flag that had been draped across his coffin
and handed it to my mother. We all said our good-byes

to Papa, and everyone walked away, except for my sisters and me. We held each other's hands tightly and started to cry. We knew our lives were going to be very different. Without our father in the business and our mother growing older as well, the business was going to be left to the three of us and our sons.

The boys came and escorted their grandmother to the car; she was very frail. The previous couple of months taking care of Papa were not easy for her. After my sisters and I finished saying our good-byes, we walked away with wonderful memories that we would cherish for all eternity. Everyone who attended the funeral had lunch at one of our favorite restaurants.

Then we began a new page in life for the first time without Cosmo Avellino.

After Papa's death, we walked around as if we were lost. One day, my sisters and I decided to go back to our old neighborhood. My mother and father had started their lives in Brooklyn. It was the place to live back in the early 1950s. The streets were clean and tree-lined, and the air seemed fresher. I remember my parents would sit across the street under a huge oak tree and talk to all the neighbors, friends, and family. My mother's brother, Uncle Pete, and his wife, Aunt Rosa, would often come over. And of course my mother's sister, Aunt Grace, would walk over and join them. They were always happy times on Elm Avenue, a far cry from what the old neighborhood became. For God's sake, the tree was gone. Something changed the world into a melting pot. The changing face

of our nation was hard to get used to. Nevertheless, we
wanted to look, so off we went. Our small street was Elm
Avenue. It was off of Coney Island Avenue in the Midwood
section of Brooklyn. Tears came to my eyes as we passed
the house we all grew up in. It was hard to believe that we
came from the broken-down house our parents took such
pride in owning. The people who were there now had no
pride in the home. The windows were so dirty and broken
that you couldn't even see through them. The porch was
all destroyed. We were in a nightmare. The sidewalk was
dirty, with paper and bottles thrown all over the streets;
it looked awful. We all looked at one another in aston-
ishment, and all at the same time said, "Papa would not
believe what it looks like now."

As we stood there, we all said to one another, "Maybe
it's better to let the past die. We wanted to return to the
small restaurant we often ate in. Well, that was closed. The
thing that amazed us was the people we saw were from all
over the world. It was as if it was Halloween. Women wore
long skirts, men wore huge hats, and some people wore
rags wrapped around their heads. We wanted to get in my
car and zoom as fast as we could. That wonderful place that
held so many pleasant memories for all of us was gone.

Back in the car, we were all quiet. We were at a loss for
words because that was the last time we ever went back
there. The past was over. As I glanced out the window,
I started to cry. Part of me wanted the house to be as it
was when we lived there, but that was gone. The tree that
my father would sit under on the weekends as he would

smoke his cigar was gone. All that was left intact on that street was the street sign that read "Elm Avenue." Isabella, Francesca, and I were happy we made the trip but sad to see what had happened to our old neighborhood.

The next day, our sons wanted to know about the house and the neighborhood. The three of us just shook our heads and did not know how to answer our sons. All I said was, "It's a far cry from how we live now." Living in the city was grand. Our boys were spoiled rotten; they worked hard and played harder. They did not know what a small house tucked away in Brooklyn was like; they had a house in the Hamptons. We also had a house upstate and a house in Florida. What a life they had; they were lucky. Papa and my mother made all of it possible for them, for us, for the family. A smile came across my face. As I sat back in my office, I thought, *I must appreciate my life each and every day.* But then, an instant fear came over me when I said the words "my life." Was I in the right place and time in life? I never felt like I belonged. When and how would I figure all this out?

As I sat in my, office I heard Tony calling me through my open door. I looked up at him as he stood in front of my huge mahogany desk that he had just bought for my office. "Nothing is too good for my Sofia," he would always tell me.

"Yes, Tony. What is it, my darling?"

He replied, "Did you hear from Marcello this morning?" I got nervous and wondered if something was wrong. He could see fear in my face.

Before I said anything, he said, "Don't worry, Sofia. Nothing is wrong. Everything is good—great, for that matter." He was waving what looked like airline tickets in my face with a huge smile.

"What is this all about?" I asked.

"We are off to Hollywood."

I jumped up and ran to him. "Tell me more! What's cookin'?"

"Sofia, wonderful news! Marcello is getting a huge award for one of his films, and we are all going to the celebration." Oh my God. I was so thrilled!

"Who do you mean by 'all'? Who is coming?" Tony said he bought half the seats on the plane, and whoever wanted to go would join us. I knew that one day, Marcello would be a big hit. He had a super talent, and I knew that one day, he would get the recognition he deserved. Tony was just as excited as I was. He told me that we were going to spend a few extra days in Beverly Hills with his son and his family. They were flying in for the awards show, and then we were all going off to the Beverly Hills Hotel to spend a relaxing weekend with all the kids.

All about Mama

As I sat at my desk, suddenly I wanted to get out of the office and go over to see my mother. I rang Francesca's phone to see if she was free, but she had an appointment and was unable to go with me. I then called Isabella. She had someone coming in, so I told them both that I would be at Mama's if they needed me. The weather was chilly, and the season was changing; soon we would have snow. I wanted to go spend some time with my mother, so I called her and told her I was walking over. She sounded like she needed some company. Mom was eighty years old now. When she was in the office, I saw her more, but now she was home all the time. For the previous seven years, she barely went to the office at all anymore. She would call from time to time just to feel like she was still part of the working family. When my mother was young, she was dynamic, full of energy. She used to keep my father on his toes. She was an extraordinary woman.

As I continued walking and the cold weather hit my face, my mind drifted to Frank, almost as if he were trying to reach me to send me a message. I knew I shouldn't be afraid of the spirit of my first husband, yet it made me feel so weird. The love Frank and I shared from the beginning to the end, I will never, ever forget.

I was almost at the building; the doorman saw me coming. He had a big smile on his face. He was always glad to see me. "You look beautiful, Sofia." My mother was waiting for me with a nice lunch that I could smell as I entered the elevator. As the elevator doors opened, my mother was already in the foyer waiting for me.

My parents' apartment was truly unbelievable. As I mentioned, my mother had a flair for decorating. When Papa was alive, he used to love to see her talents. "Sofia, Sofia, come in the kitchen with me." We all loved to sit in the kitchen and enjoyed just talking. My mother's lunch was great. She made the best eggplant in the country. The coffee was on, and she loved to cook for all of us. Even though she had a complete staff to help her, she still did her own cooking. We had a nice afternoon just sitting and talking about everything; it was a nice mother–daughter chat. "Before you leave, Sofia, I have to tell you something." My mother looked up at me with fear in her eyes and said, "I have to go to the doctor."

I wasn't sure why she was so upset, so I reassured her that I or one of my sisters would get her there. She looked back at me, and with her eyes filling with tears, she said, "No, Sofia. I have cancer." Well, now everything stopped. The beautiful blue sky turned dark gray in my heart. Tears flooded my eyes, and my heart was racing faster than the thoughts in my head. I stood up and looked at her with confusion; I just didn't understand.

"Sofia, last week I went to the doctor because I wasn't feeling well. He did many tests, and they found out that I have stomach cancer. I'm not going to take chemotherapy and put all that poison in my system." Well, she knew that I wasn't going to go for that.

I said, "Oh yes you are!"

She quickly replied, "Sofia, you're not making me do something that I don't want to do."

I pleaded with her. "With the medicine they have today, you can get better and live another ten years!"

My mother was so frustrated with me and said, "What am I going to do here for ten more years? I want to go and be with Papa. You girls are all grown women. Everybody is doing well, and I have nothing do here anymore. You have to just let me go."

We argued for about another fifteen minutes, and she finally decided that she would get at least some treatment. She might have done it just to shut me up and make me happy. Well, it did shut me up, and I was happy. I decided that we needed to stop talking about cancer and end the afternoon with a cup of coffee.

I thought this was going to be such a lovely day, but then my afternoon turned out worse than I could have imagined. So terrible, such awful news. My job now was to tell the girls. I told my mother that I was going back to the office and I would be back later with the girls. I think she was happy that she had finally told me. I got back to work, called my sisters into my office, and gave them the awful news. They were all startled and scared, and the look of fear was in their eyes. The days moved very quickly. We were with Mama each day, back and forth to the doctors, NYU, Sloan-Kettering—anywhere we thought the best doctor would be. Mama had the best of care and finally had a few treatments. The truth is, she did feel a little better, and for a few months, she was even smiling again.

The kids were always around her, and we kept her busy to get her mind off all of it. Summer turned to fall, and once again it was winter. The months seemed to fly by. On a cold Saturday morning in January, Tony and I went over to see Mama, and she was very weak. The few months that she felt better were quickly behind us; time was slipping away. Tony and I picked up a few bagels and met Isabella at Mama's apartment. Isabella was going to the gym and stopped by on her way. When I got there, Isabella's face showed that something was wrong. "Mommy is losing it. She's not good at all, and she's just lifeless today. Go try to talk to her."

I went in and sat with Mama while she drifted in and out of sleep. The doctor and the nurse had just left and would be back in a few hours to check on her. When Mama was finally able to open her eyes, I asked her how she was feeling. She looked annoyed at me for asking her that. I just smiled at her. She wanted to sit up so we could talk, so I helped her a bit. "Sofia, I have to tell you something. I have to tell you now because I am running out of time."

I took her hand in mine and said "OK, Mama, I am here to listen."

My mother was so frail, and her hands were so thin; even her voice was different. Cancer is devastation. It was such a heartache to watch Mama go through it and such a painful way to leave this earth. My mother was such a strong, beautiful woman for her whole life, and now she was down to just ninety pounds. Her hair was so thin and her body so frail. She lay there looking so pitiful. I tried to make her laugh now and then, but it wasn't working anymore.

Mama said to me, "Sofia, close the door. I have to talk to you." My heart was pounding. I thought, *What's wrong with you? Sofia, this is your mother, why are you so nervous?* I tried to calm myself down, and my mom tried to lift herself up on her pillow. I helped her, and she sat up.

"Sofia, open the window. Move the curtain, I want to see the daylight." I got off the chair and did as she instructed. When I turned around to look at her, I could barely hold back my tears. I knew the days were numbered and that my mother was leaving us shortly. I pulled myself together and walked over to the bed. I sat in the chair next to her. At first, she was silent. Then she began to talk to me. "Sofia, when you were a little girl, believe it or not, you were taken from Papa and me." Not believing what I was hearing, I said, "What? How come I never knew this?"

She said, "Papa and I decided not to tell you. It happened when you were just a baby. It was a beautiful spring day, and I had gone into a store to buy ribbons for your hair. When I came out, the carriage was gone. I was yelling and screaming in the street. At the time, the police were on horses. I was outside the store yelling, and one of the officers galloped over on his horse. I told him, 'Please, please help me! Someone took my daughter. Someone took my baby!' It seemed like the whole city stopped for a brief moment. What seemed like hours was just minutes. The police got you back very quickly. An old woman had taken you, and she turned you over in the carriage and was taking you into her house."

My mother said she was breathless and felt like she had been hit by a truck. "All I wanted was to get you home. It was a day I will never forget." My eyes were wide open, and my ears were pinned to every word from Mama. I couldn't even imagine what I was going to hear next.

"The rest of my life, I never left my babies unattended," Mama said. "It was a terrible ordeal."

I said, "Mama, how could I have not been told this story? It's amazing! Was it in the newspaper? Did you press charges? Did you see the woman who took me?"

My mother was a peaceful soul; she did not want any attention and was just happy to get me back. The press, the news, photographs—that was not her style. I thought the story was over, and she had nothing left to tell me, but that was not the case.

"Sofia, sit back down; there's more." She went on to tell me that I was so beautiful. She said she and Papa were very proud of me and that she loved me with all her heart. She said, "Sofia, you're right. You are different. A year after you were taken, I received a phone call from someone I did not know. At the other end of the phone was a very soft-spoken woman. Right away she knew my name and said, 'Frances

Avellino, I'd like to meet with you.' When I asked her who she was, she said, 'Please don't ask me any questions on the phone, I need to meet you. It can be anywhere in the city, but you have to go alone.' I would usually never do anything like that, Sofia, but I felt compelled to listen to her, and much to my surprise, I wanted to. She gave me a date and time, and she said to be in the Water Club. When I asked how I would know her, she said she knew me. I hung up the phone, and when Papa came home that night, I told him. He was mad at me and asked, 'What does that mean? It must be a crazy lady!' Papa told me that I wasn't to go anywhere. He said I could not go. Something told me that I had to go, and I didn't care if he came with me or not. It was the afternoon, and nobody was going to hurt me in the middle of the Water Club. I said, 'If you do not come, I'm going alone.' Papa didn't understand why I would want to go to meet a complete stranger, a lady I didn't know anything about. What did she want? Money? Maybe she was going kill me. I didn't know why, but I wanted to go. I knew I had to. When I got there, I stood around for a few minutes, and then a woman approached me. She handed me a box and said, 'This belongs to Sofia. It will explain her life."

Mama was so exhausted. She fell asleep and never uttered another word about this. I was so taken aback with all I just heard; I just left and let my mother sleep.

My mother's cancer was taking over. Each day she grew weaker and weaker. That strong, beautiful face she once had was long gone. She had a hard time just opening her eyes. However, when she heard the family was coming, she would try to smile. It was hard when we lost Papa, and this was going to be even harder. Once our mother was gone, we would be all alone.

We were faced with handling the business and the properties; we had a lot to take care of. None of us wanted to let the apartment go; we all loved it. When the time came, we had the idea for our Aunt Rosa to live in the apartment. She had always wanted to live in the city. She was in her seventies and in no way looked it or even acted it; she was very young at heart.

She was living in Park Slope at the time, and I thought she would love to be right in the city. I knew she would take good care of the apartment. We could have just sold the apartment, after all, but knowing that a family member would live there made us all feel a little better. We could get a fortune for such a great place, but money was not an issue. No rent was needed; we would all talk when the time came, and that time was right in front of us.

It was about five o'clock on a Sunday afternoon. My two sisters were in the living room. Roberto and Justin were over to see their Mema, as they called her. The coffee was on, and it was starting to get dark outside. Francesca and Isabella were still over. We were waiting for the grandkids to come.

The apartment was four thousand square feet, which was huge, especially for a place in the city. Our parents even had a playroom for their great-grandchildren. It was wonderful to be all together.

The nurse came from the bedroom and said, "Sofia, your mother wants you." When I walked into the room, my mother was sitting up, and she did look good. She was always a beautiful lady and had a smile that was worth millions. As I sat in the chair, my mother said to open the drawer on the side of the bed. So I did as she asked, and in the drawer was a book. I reached for it, and it looked like a journal. My mother took my hand and said, "Sofia, once I die, you open it, and it will change your life." When I heard her say "die," I started to cry. My mother took my hand and was holding on to me so tightly. Her eyes were dark and so sad, and she knew her beautiful life was slipping away.

My son, Cosmo, was now heading over. He was the firstborn and boy, did my mother worship the ground he walked on. He was the sunshine of her life. His eyes always filled with tears when he would see her in bed so sick. Joseph, Jamie, Justin, and Richard were on their way over, too. My Marcello was not in town, but he would make sure to call me each day to check in. All the boys had a special place for their grandmother.

Losing parents, grandparents, anyone is just so hard. We were all facing that now. I was still sitting with Mama, and she said, "Sofia, I love you very much. You know that you are my daughter, no matter what?"

Now, what was that supposed to mean to me? What was Mama talking about? Was she talking crazy because of the drugs? She looked at me repeatedly with tears in her eyes.

I said, "I love you, Mama."

She looked back at me. "Once I am gone, Sofia, you will finally find out the truth. Just remember that Papa and I always have and always will love you."

I turned and saw that the girls were there. Isabella said, "Is this a private party, Mommy?" She smiled, and we all sat on the bed.

We made her smile. She looked at all of us and said, "My girls, you are just the best ladies in town."

In my heart, I thought maybe it was the last time we would all be with her. That night, we all went home and started to settle in and get ready for work on Monday. At about midnight, my phone rang. It was Francesca. "Sofia, Sofia, Sofia. Mama, it's...over. Mama's gone..."

I dropped to the floor and started crying. Tony came running to make sure I was OK and to comfort me. Francesca and Isabella were going over to the apartment, and I said I would meet them there. The house felt cold and dark; we all walked in at the same time. We cried in each other's arms for a while. Then it was time to go into the bedroom. It was time to say good-bye to our mother. Frances Maria Billera Avellino was gone. I walked in first. Mama looked so peaceful; she looked beautiful. She had a smirk on her face, as if she saw Papa and they were finally together again. I am a person of faith, and I knew that happened. Our family priest came over at 1:30 a.m. The house was full; all the boys came, and it was a sad night for our family. The housekeeper was crying, and the doorman came up. Frances was loved by all. We talked with the priest for a few hours and planned an elaborate funeral for our mother because she so deserved it. The funeral would last for two days, and then she would be in her final resting place, where she belongs, right next to Papa.

The wake was so busy, with so many people. Wall to wall, there were about one hundred floral arrangements. People were everywhere. My sisters and I sat in the front, near the coffin, and greeted everyone; it was a long, hard two days. Then the final morning arrived. We went back to the funeral parlor before they closed the coffin and looked at our mother for the very last time. The tears flooded our eyes as we held on to each other. Isabella, Francesca, and I were drained. We wanted our parents back, but we all knew that it was out of the question. Justin said a few beautiful words as he stood in front of the coffin with tears rolling down his face. All the boys were now crying. The limo drivers came in to get us girls. We didn't want to leave our mother. We did not want to close the coffin. We did not want to accept reality—our mother was no longer with us.

The church was so beautiful, as were the music, the people, and the words the priest spoke. Wall to wall, not a seat was empty. Francesca, Isabella, and I, along with our families, walked in, dressed in black, with our broken hearts behind the coffin. The mass was over, and off we went into the cars. It was a long ride. We all sat quietly, lost in our thoughts. It was difficult to even get out of the car to say our final good-byes and watch them lower the coffin into the ground.

It was a gorgeous, sunny day. As my sisters and I held each other, we realized that life would never be the same. Yes, we had our grandchildren and would share in much joy, and we were healthy and still all working. But with our parents both gone, we all had a huge hole in our lives and hearts.

Life will go on...

Christmas with the Avellino Family

IT WAS THAT wonderful time of the year—Christmas. A time of joy and peace, a time to celebrate the birth of Jesus. The stores were all jumping; people were hustling to get all their last-minute gifts. People everywhere were in a good mood. Nothing was going to bother anyone this time of year; peace and harmony for all the world. Yet it did not close the huge hole my sisters and I had in our hearts because our parents were not with us anymore. This was the first Christmas without Mama and Papa, so it was going to be quite different. Yes, we had each other and all the kids to keep us busy. We were still going up to our parents' apartment. Aunt Rosa was now living there and was excited to have all of us over for the holiday. We all planned a delicious menu, and Charles would cook a few of his favorite things. In all, we had seven different types of fish; that was the tradition in our house. Aunt Rosa had the apartment decorated so beautifully. She couldn't wait for Christmas Eve for us to all get there and see it.

Every year, my sisters and I set aside one day to take all the grandkids shopping. Even though Isabella still had no grandchildren, she would not miss it for the world; she loved to shop and spoil all the kids. Francesca and I had been doing that for years, and the kids looked so forward to it. We would start the day with a big, healthy breakfast, and then off we went to shop. The kids could not be happier. "Nana, how about this? How about that?" Francesca's girls were doing the same thing. Her girls called her "Grandmamma," so all over the busy store, we heard our grandchildren call for us in all directions. They loved buying gifts for their parents, teachers, and each other—the sky was the limit. It was a great tradition, and we all loved it.

When we finally finished, we had bags and boxes all over the place. We had a ball. We went back to our apartment, where Tony ordered food for us to enjoy, and soon the grandchildren would be picked up. It was truly a happy season, and we were all excited to spend it in our parents' apartment. It was sad and happy all rolled into one. The days went flying by, and finally it was Christmas Eve. It was a snowy, December afternoon, and we were all excited to see the snowfall. We started to head over and get ready for our fabulous Christmas Eve dinner. The kids would start asking us at seven if they could open just one gift—every year was the same. When we all settled in, some of the kids were running around, happy to be together, and some of the family members were sitting, looking at old pictures. While everyone was busy, I disappeared into my parents' bedroom. I closed my eyes and wished to see my mother and father just one more time. I started to open the drawers to see if I could discover anything more about myself. I never did open that book Mama had handed me only months before. I told myself that after the New Year, I was going to open the book. It was at the top of my things-to-do list. I was looking through my mother's things when I came across a box. It looked like a shoebox. I instantly started to cry when I opened it. What was this all about? In it were many pieces of paper my mother had started to write to me. I sat on the bed and read them over and over again.

Dear Sofia,

This is so hard for me to talk about, so I thought if I wrote it, it might be easier. Sofia, your father and I love you so very much, and I hope one day you will understand all this.

I was so confused because I knew all the details of my kidnapping and the other things that went on, so what the hell else could this be? My mother had stopped writing after those two lines on almost every paper. I sat on the bed with my eyes closed, wondering what else I would find out. It was Christmas Eve and I wanted to enjoy my family and all the good food. Just then, the door swung open, and my grandson, Nicky, flew in. "Nana, we want to watch a Christmas movie. Can we go into the movie room?"

I smiled and said, "Do whatever you want. It's Christmas Eve." I walked out of the bedroom and I was thrilled that I had my family all around me to enjoy this night.

The evening was moving along very smoothly. Joseph then stood up and said he had a surprise for all of us. Our thoughts immediately went to Sabrina—could she be having another baby? No, that was not it. Joseph was having a new home built in Chappaqua, New York. A few years earlier, Cosmo had bought a house in the neighboring town, and Joseph loved it. He had many photos for us to look at; the house was magnificent. He and Sabrina could not wait for all of us to get up there to see it. It was a beautiful Christmas surprise to add to Christmas Eve dinner.

We ate for hours on end. The food never stopped coming, and all of it was so good. Finally, the dishes were cleared, and we started to set the table for dessert. The kids were so excited to start to open all their gifts, and the night was sensational. There were papers, boxes, and bows everywhere. Around one, we all gathered our belongings and Christmas presents and went home. On Christmas Day, we all stayed in our own homes and enjoyed the peace and quiet. All our sons went to spend the day with their in-laws, so Tony and I just sat back, all alone, and enjoyed Christmas together. It was a beautiful Christmas holiday, and we got through it all together.

The next day, Tony and I headed to Florida to share the rest of the Christmas season with his family. We enjoyed the week there and stayed with them until right after the New Year. It was the only time we would close our offices and give everyone extra vacation time. We could enjoy being in Florida, relaxed, and not have to worry about the office. Soon, we would say good-bye to the year and hope and pray that only love, peace, and happy times were ahead for the Avellino family.

The Wedding

— ❦ —

ONE NIGHT, TONY and I were relaxing home in front of the fire when the doorman called up to tell us that Marcello was coming up with Willow. What a great surprise! I was so happy to see them; they were always a pleasure to be around. We all sat around for a while talking. I noticed that Marcello was acting nervous, doing his usual pacing back and forth. I knew how he would get before a film release, so I was waiting to hear about a film. Suddenly, Marcello stood up and said, "Mom, Tony, do you have any champagne?" Tony got up, went over to the bar, and got out the glasses and the bottle of Cristal. He said, "Of course we do. What's the occasion?"

Marcello started to talk. I was waiting for him to tell me he was up for an Oscar. Well, the news was much more exciting. He said, "We want to plan our wedding."

Willow said, "We called my parents in Australia, and they were thrilled."

Oh my God! I jumped up and was so happy for them. The kisses and hugs were running wild. They wanted a wedding in May, only a few months away, but because we knew half of Manhattan, we could do it with ease. I asked, "So where do you want to have the wedding?"

Marcello replied, "Willow and I decided to let you both choose the location. Any place is fine with us. We trust your judgment."

I said, "Hmm. Let's see, how about the Ritz-Carlton, in Soho? We all love that place. I will call Tracey in the morning. She is the coordinator for the Ritz and will help us."

Willow said to me, "There is just one thing I must have, Sofia."

I said, "Anything you two want is yours. Make sure you tell your parents that the wedding is a gift from Tony and me."

"That would be so wonderful!" she replied. "The one thing I have wanted since I moved to New York is a horse and carriage to take us to the church."

I said, "That's a marvelous idea. I love it. I will call and have everything arranged. The Avellino family will get it all done. Now, for your dress, my darling daughter-in-law, how about Valentino? When will your parents get in?"

"They will be coming one to two weeks before the wedding."

I told Willow, "They can stay with us or at the Ritz; I will arrange it."

Willow said her sister would go gown hunting with her. Willow's twin sister, Brooke, was living in Manhattan and working for the HGTV network. She was a darling girl, so much like Willow. "Just tell me when you want to go, and I will arrange any showroom that you want." I was so excited that I couldn't see straight. My Marcello was going to be a married man! Marcello would never roam far from me; he was my youngest, and I still had him under my wing.

He and I were in the kitchen for a few minutes, getting some food to snack on. He saw the tears running down my face. "Mom," he said, "what would I do without you? I love you so much for all you do for me. You have always made my life so much easier. I am forever grateful, Mother. You are truly the best."

I could not hold back my tears of joy. "Marcello, you've always made me so proud. You and your brothers are my life. Anything I can do, I will. My sons come first in my life. I always pray that the women you have all chosen realize how special you are."

All night we sat around and talked and laughed and planned the Saturday-night wedding for May, only a few months away. We had a huge staff, so we could make anything happen.

The following night, we all went out to eat with the family. Marcello and Willow told everyone the exciting news, and they were all thrilled. As time ticked away, we were getting ready for the big wedding. Joseph and Cosmo were his best men. All the kids in the family were going to be in the procession at Saint Patrick's Cathedral. They would arrive in a second horse and buggy, leading the bride and groom. The rest of the family, all the cousins, would walk the guests into the church. Willow's sister, Brooke, would be her maid of honor. The wedding was going to be simple but very classy. The guest list was around four hundred. Would you call that simple? The Avellino family was very well known in Manhattan, and many people wanted to attend. It was going to be the wedding of the year. My sisters and I were going into and out of showrooms looking for the right dress. Sometimes, designers would call us and bring their line up to the office. We had a blast shopping for dresses.

It was already April, and the wedding was almost here. Each day, we got a little closer to the big day. The boys took Marcello out on the town; they did not leave Manhattan. The girls took Willow out one night. Willow and Brooke's parents would be here in just a few days. We did not have a rehearsal dinner because Marcello and Willow did not want one.

Time flew by, and finally, it was the night before the wedding. I was a nervous wreck, yet so damn happy. That night, I lay in Tony's arms, wishing that my parents were still with us. Frank's family was all gone, too; just one aunt was still around, and she did RSVP for the wedding. It was a heartbreak that Frank never got to see any of his children get married. Life is bittersweet. Thank God, my parents taught us to move forward and handle whatever life hits us with.

Putting the wedding together ran very smoothly. I had lots of help. Willow and Marcello were so easy; they were both on cloud nine and busy with all the other details. After the wedding, they were moving to a bigger apartment in Manhattan and busy looking for just the right place. The honeymoon was going to be in Italy and then on to London.

It was all going to be a dream come true. Tony's sons were coming in for the weekend. We did not miss a beat.

After meeting Willow's parents, I could see why she was so sweet. I will tell you, they got the biggest kick out of us. We were nothing like their quiet existence in Australia. The morning of the wedding, we had a police escort all the way to St. Patrick's Cathedral. Willow, Brooke, and their parents were in the carriage. The cathedral was a dream with flowers every place you looked. The music selection was beautiful. We were all waiting for the bride. When the carriage horses came galloping down the block, my heart stopped. That strange woman I saw only months ago who startled me at the family party is now here today. Why do I have these odd feelings about a perfect stranger? Why was this woman there to haunt me on one of most exciting days of my life? I was not going to allow her to interrupt my joy.

The sun was shining so brightly, and the sky was so blue that it almost looked make-believe, like a fairytale. The doors of the cathedral opened, and I walked in with Tony on my arm. I felt like a billion dollars. My dress was elegant, sexy, and simply gorgeous; it was my day to be proud. All my daughters-in-law looked like they were straight out of a fashion magazine. They all looked stunning, with a beautiful glow in their smiles. We all knew this day was going to be a day to remember. Marcello was at the altar. He walked over to me with tears in his eyes. "Mom, I love you. Thank you for this wedding."

I did not want to let him go. My baby was leaving me, going to the arms of another. But I was confident she was the one for Marcello. I whispered in his ear, "Marcello, I will always be here for you." We both smiled. At that moment, the music got loud, and we all stood, turned, and watched the bride walk down that very long aisle, the newest member of the Avellino family. Willow looked out of this world, with her green eyes so wide and beautiful. Marcello stared into her eyes. Her father handed his precious daughter over to my son, and that was it for me—tears, tears, tears. Tony embraced me and held me in his arms. The ceremony was the most beautiful. Precious words were spoken, and all we heard were my sisters and me sobbing happy tears. Finally the priest said, "I now pronounce you husband and wife. You may now kiss the bride." At that moment, the church roared with overwhelming applause.

We all walked out of the church with excitement and joy for the happy couple. I stood still for a moment, stared up into the cathedral, and said a prayer for them in hopes that my parents and Frank would watch over them from the heavens.

The Ritz-Carlton was exquisite. Not even a half hour had passed, and everyone was talking, laughing, mingling, and drinking champagne. The food, the ambiance, the people, the music—it was all perfect, and Willow and Marcello were the perfect host and hostess. So many friends and family. It was such a memorable wedding; none of the guests would ever forget it. Tony and I, along with my sisters, danced the night away. All my friends and family were having a ball. It was an amazing wedding for an amazing couple. It gave me great joy to see my three sons enjoying the night, laughing, dancing, and celebrating their brother's happy event.

Congratulations, my children, and here's to the new Mr. and Mrs. Avellino and a wonderful beginning.

The Book in Question

OUR LIVES WERE not the same anymore. Mama and Papa were gone. The business was the same, but the spirit was not there anymore. When we lost our parents, my sisters and I lost a huge piece of our hearts; it would never come back. My life was busier than ever. Isabella and Francesca and I worked, worked, worked. The boys were running around the globe to create new accounts, and life was moving fast.

I never looked at that book my mother put in my hand the day she passed away. It was now time for me to do that. I spoke with Tony about my looking in the book. I had a great fear about finding out the unknown. What was I afraid of? Maybe just the fear itself. I knew I had to find out. The time was now—no more procrastinating. Now that my mother was gone, the day was here. I opened the book that she had handed me on her deathbed, and I knew I must face my life and get it over with.

Tony was with me, and we sat there looking into each other's eyes, wondering what lay ahead for us, not having a clue what this book meant. Right before Mom died, she sat me down and told me to take the book and open it after some time had passed, so I did just that. Inside was a white envelope. I was tempted to open it, but I did not have the courage to unveil what was inside. So many thoughts were racing through my mind. My hands were shaking, and my head was spinning. The minutes were ticking. I was so nervous. I looked at Tony and said, "OK, my love, this is it." There was nothing in the book; it was just an empty book—blank pages and a white envelope. Perhaps my mother wanted me to write in it after the truth was revealed. What was I about to find out? Again, I looked at Tony and said, "Should I open the envelope?"

He looked at me with love and affection, took my hand in his, and said, "Yes, my love, it's time. You must know the truth after all these years." Maybe we will be surprised; it might just be simple. As the clock was ticking, it was ten o'clock now, so I took the envelope in my hand and as carefully as can be.

All that was inside was a number that appeared to be a telephone number. There was no name, no explanation, nothing. Just a number, and at that split second, I was angry with my mother. Was she playing a game with me? Now what was I to do? I still had no answer—nothing but a phone number with an area code I wasn't familiar with. I gave Tony the area code, and he shouted out, "There's no such area code!" I asked him if I should call now, but we decided it was too late to call. We went to bed because there was just too much to digest for one night to start thinking about anything else. I decided I would call the next day, or maybe in a few days. Tony always knew the right things to say to me. He was the sweetest man on earth and knew how to make me feel better and to make me love him more.

That night as I lay in bed, my mind was all over the place. What would this phone number reveal? Maybe I would finally find out who I was. My mother must have had a reason for keeping it a mystery. I know that within days I would find out. I was not going to call in the morning; I was very busy at work. The kids were going to come over for the weekend, and Marcello and Willow were coming home from LA. All my boys were married now. Marcello had a few films in various theaters around the city. I was so proud of him. Film had been his life since he was a young child, and God bless him. He was soon going to be thirty-two years old—not really my baby anymore, but in my eyes he would always be my baby. His plane landed early on Saturday morning, and our driver would go pick him and Willow up. On Sunday, the entire family would come for a nice Sunday dinner.

With my husband, Frank, dying so early in life, I still wanted to raise my boys so he would be proud, and I did just that. Until Tony, I wandered around for many years not attached to anyone; my family and my boys were my life. I had many wonderful, close friends, but my children and grandchildren would always come first. That was the strong Italian family we came from.

I feared that the envelope and the phone number might change all that. I was not going to think about it anymore; the weekend was here, and I wanted to enjoy the kids. Tony so loved my family. His sons adored him, and his girls—his granddaughters—were his life. Both girls attended Columbia University and saw us as often as they can. In the summer months, we put them to work. We were always around his children; they both lived in Florida. His youngest son was thinking of moving to Las Vegas to open up a new business. Tony was glad to hear that because Vegas was his favorite town. His daughter-in-law, Laura, and I had a warm and friendly connection. I often wondered if that would change after we found out the truth about Sofia.

Am I Dreaming?

———— ❧❧ ————

I HAD TO admit, the phone call I was about to make scared me to death. I knew I was different, and now I was ready to see why. I always thought I was extremely brave and lived my life with courage and grace. Let's face it—we are ultimately the only ones in charge of our own lives, and it was now time for me to do what needed to be done. Maybe I was about to face something unique in my life, a new discovery. The wind was pulling under my wings, and I had to soar. I had to get to the bottom of this, and today was the day.

After I finally made the phone call, I had to meet a mystery lady in the park. What was I looking for? Who would be there? I knew something was going to happen. My anticipation was so overwhelming, I thought I would faint. The lady on the phone instructed me to meet her by the stables. My mind suddenly wandered back to the night of the party, when I saw the stunning white horse with that strange woman riding it. Was this all connected?

It was a beautiful day, with the sun was shining so brightly. The wind was fast and furious. It was a special spring day, and Central Park was so pleasant. I walked slowly, and my heart was beating wildly. I could not understand all this. Was this for real? It was 2004. What was all this mystery about who I was? What was going to happen? I saw the cherry trees from a distance but could not see anyone there; this area of the park was so isolated. For a second, I was frozen. Maybe I was heading right into danger. Maybe today I would die. Was someone waiting there to kill me? My mind was racing. I had a hundred things in my head that could happen to me. But I was there now and not going back. Maybe my twisted mind would be settled after this meeting. All the days and nights, not knowing why I felt so out of place in my own skin, would end.

Why was I always seeing and feeling things that no one else did? Why did I have platelet counts that were so low? I was diagnosed with a blood disorder that all the high-profile doctors in Manhattan would tell me was absolutely hereditary, yet not one person in my family had anything wrong with their blood, as far back as I could search. Whenever I would ask my mother, she would say that the doctors were wrong. Nevertheless, the facts were that I had a blood problem and couldn't figure out exactly how I got it. So if it was hereditary, whose family was I connected to? Most people with this low count wouldn't be walking around, yet there I was.

Why, why, why? All those questions, and never did I get an answer. Tony understood me so well. He knew me and was always there to comfort me. I was a lucky lady, having two fabulous, good, caring men in my life. Some women never get the chance to have one. My mind was going in all directions—my family and my friends, all there in my head. I needed to find some answers.

From the corner of my eye, I thought I saw something, I turned and saw that it was there, but then gone. Was this a joke?

I stood perfectly still and was looking in all directions to find something, or someone. Then I saw the most elegant white horse. I instantly flashed back once again to the night of the party, and it did look like the same horse I saw that night. It looked like it was glistening in the sunlight. As it came closer, a strange feeling took over me, as if I knew both the horse and the person on it. It was amazing. Riding the horse was a young woman with long, wavy hair. I saw her smile from yards away. Oh my, she looked very much like me when I was young. Now I knew, this was some kind of crazy dream. I was downright scared. I wanted to run out of the park to my apartment and lock myself in. But I didn't. My body was frozen, so I could not move. The horse was getting closer and closer, and soon it was right in front of me. I heard my name: "Sofia. Sofia, come over to me."

It sounded musical. I still could not move. It felt like I was in the middle of a sci-fi movie. What the hell was this about? I took a very deep breath and looked up at the lady. She got off the horse, walked closer to me, and held out her hand. She said, "Let me take you home." The next thing I knew, all the trees around me were sparkling and shining. I couldn't help but wonder, *What's going to happen to me now? Did I die and go to heaven?*

There I was, faced with what I thought was a dream. It was true: things you just cannot imagine *can happen.* Instantly, a strange, overwhelming feeling ran through me: I was home.

Maybe I was on another planet. From what I saw at a glance, the place seemed ideal. It was clean and so picture-perfect, as if I were in a painting.

I stood there in this very strange place in shock. The houses were all so pretty, in white, yellow, pink, and blue. It looked to me like every five or six homes had their own park and pool. It was just overpowering. With palm trees blowing in the mild wind, I felt so strange and out of place. I stood there and wondered, *How can I explain this to anyone when I can't believe it, and it's in front of me?* The cars were nothing like I'd seen before. They were clear, Lucite—I could see right through them. They were all a funny shape and hovered over the street. The water was so clear; it was better than any ocean I'd ever seen.

I was not in Central Park anymore, but I wasn't sure where I really was or how I got there. The next thing I knew, two people were approaching me. As they got closer, my fear grew more intense. They held out their hands and said, "Welcome home, Sofia."

At that point, I wanted to jump out of my skin. "This is not my home!" I said. "Who are you?" Even though I was scared and confused, I felt comfortable in their presence and knew instantly that I had a connection to them. The two people who were speaking to me explained that they were my birth parents. I was so scared, yet, as I looked up at them,

I could see that the woman was a pretty lady with a bright smile, and the man looked so distinguished. Both of them were dressed so fancy, and in the back of my mind, I knew I had a connection to these strangers. My mother had beautiful, light eyes, a mirror to my own. There was definitely a family resemblance, something I had never felt before in my life. These two people looked more like me than the mother and father who had raised me. Now I began to shake, and even more fear came over me. I was in total shock. If I wasn't in heaven, then maybe this was hell. I needed more information; I needed details. I just wanted to go home, but how the hell would I get there?

They started to explain to me what had happened on that day when I was kidnapped forty-nine years earlier, like the morning Mama explained to me when she took her last breath. I couldn't think straight. Why would they switch me? Why wouldn't they want me as a baby? They had a warm and friendly charm that I felt comfortable with. They spoke in such a soft tone; it was so relaxing and calming to listen to them. They explained that yes, my name was Sofia Avellino, and I was raised in New York, but that was not where I was born. On that day forty-nine years earlier, the *Land of Lavasa* came down and made a switch. Who they choose was random. Why did they do it? No one really knew. I realized that the lady on the horse was the real Sofia whom Mama and Papa gave birth to. Everything I saw and everything I heard was so overwhelming, I didn't think anything else could shock me. How wrong I was. Little did I know what I was about to encounter. In the distance, I saw a man approaching. His body was a blurry silhouette, like a camera that needs to be focused. As he got closer, it became much clearer. Oh my God! It was my husband, whom I thought had passed away ten years earlier.

Now my Frank was standing in front of me. How was he there in Lavasa? That did it! Now I knew I was in heaven. I wanted to run and fall into his arms, but something stopped me. With tears rolling down my face, I put my hands up and yelled, "Stop this! I can't take it. What is going on? Frank, why am I here? Why did I die?"

I was furious, nervous, scared, and frustrated all rolled into one.

Frank said, "Sofia, calm down. Take a deep breath and listen to me."

With that, he put his arm around me, and we walked to a gorgeous garden and sat in a gazebo. It was so tranquil, calm, and peaceful. I felt so good for a brief moment. Everywhere I looked, colorful flowers surrounded us. He grabbed me and kissed me. The warm, wonderful, sexual love and passion all came back to life. We stared into each other's eyes, and I just couldn't believe I was back in the arms of my first husband. I couldn't take a chance on losing him again. There I was, in Frank's arms, but what about my Tony? It was like a piercing pain to my heart.

"Frank, I asked you a question. Am I in heaven with you?"

Frank finally replied, "First and foremost, you are still alive, my darling. I want you to stay here and live with me,

Sofia, but I know your devotion to our children and our grandchildren will make this a difficult decision." I wanted to jump up and punch him in the face for wanting me to leave our family behind.

Frank continued, "Most people would not get the opportunity that you are offered here. Lavasa is a remarkable place to live. Yes, I miss you and our children and all we had together. I can never go back to be with you, but you, my darling Sofia, can come with me." I still didn't understand how and why Frank was even standing in front of me. He could see my confusion and anger about his presence and started to explain. "Right before I took my last breath on earth, the enchanted people of Lavasa brought me here so that when the time came, I would help explain to you what Lavasa is and convince you to stay."

I stood there shaking my head, screaming that this could not be. "Please, someone, wake me up! I really must be dreaming." Frank put his arms around me and cried along with me. He whispered in my ear, "I love you and always will."

I wanted to push him away from me and say, "How dare you do this to me!" Something stopped me; the words couldn't come out of my mouth. I really could not believe I was there with Frank. Lavasa sounded wonderful—but how sensational can it be if you leave behind your legacy? If I made the decision to leave earth, I would be leaving behind my children, my grandchildren, my Tony. Frank was the first love of my life, but I didn't think

I could walk away from my Tony. Yes, the Land of Lavasa was enchanting—everywhere I looked, I saw nothing but amazing sights. However, all that beauty did not compare to the love I shared with your family.

No, I was not born in the Avellino family, whom I loved and admired. They did raise me, keep me safe, and give me a fantastic life. I would have the people I loved with me until my time ended. I was not changing that for anything in the world. I called out, "So to you, the Land of Lavasa, I'm sorry. I didn't get to know my real parents. Maybe I would have been different, but now there's no way I'm trading my life. I cannot start all over again. Frances and Cosmo Avellino were and are my real parents. They can rest in peace knowing I will continue the life they created for me."

When we look up in the clouds and wonder if there could be another place, take it from me, there is such a place. One day, if you ever feel that you don't belong and that you feel different from the rest, and not like everyone else, *maybe you're not!*

Now I'm Home
⊹⊱⊰⊹

AFTER I LEFT Lavasa, the next thing I knew, I was back in Central Park. How long was I gone? I felt like I was in a dream. I sat on a bench, closed my eyes, and tried to reconnect with what I had just witnessed. Was I there for minutes or hours? I had no concept of time. All I knew was that what I had seen most of my life was in front of me, just like I saw it in my dreams, my thoughts, and especially on all those plane rides. I did not know what to think. For a brief moment, I even wondered if I was an alien. Why me? I wanted answers to all my questions. Yes, my real parents did explain that Lavasa just picks people at random. There was no rhyme or reason as to how it worked. I needed to remember all that they just told me, but my head would not stop spinning.

Oh my God, now what? How many of us would change our lives if we could? Stop our lives as we knew them and continue with a fresh new start, in a different place—a place that did not have any chaos like we lived with. No terrorism, no disastrous acts of nature, no poverty. It was a place where life is a pleasant dream each day. I would describe it as living over the rainbow. The thing that

98

impressed me most was that everyone looked carefree. I could feel the comfort and energy of peace in Lavasa. If only our world was like that now. I wondered, *How can I start all over as the Sofia Avellino I always knew I was?* If I were to stay in Lavasa, the real Sofia Avellino would switch places with me, just as it was when we were both born. Tears rolled down my face. How can this be, and why me? For the first time in my life, I had a clear vision of who I was. Yes, for most of my life, the feeling of confusion and frustration had filled my days. Now, the feelings had changed. Was it better when I did not know? I just wanted to run away. How could I face everyone and tell them all this? I thought, *I am a phony. I am not who they think I am. How can I find a solution?* My parents I just met in Lavasa gave me forty-eight hours to decide. My Frank, my first husband, was in Lavasa. I wondered if I should leave my life and spend my days in Lavasa with him. No, I could not do that. Sofia Avellino had it all, or did she? Lavasa was a place that was surely out of this world. The colors of nature exploded. The air was so fresh. Feeling the warm wind on my face is just sensational. Frank, my dear husband, who passed from cancer, was there.

It was all bizarre to me. Should I run to church to sit and talk to a priest? Did I need guidance? I knew in my heart that there was no place for me but right here, but why was I so confused? Did I want to get to know my real parents? How could I walk away and start all over again? I had lost Frank years ago; he was gone. Yes, it was the thrill of a lifetime to see him again; however, he was gone from my life. The love of my life was now Tony. Would anyone really believe this? How would I tell my family? The beautiful life of Sofia had a dark cloud over it. I needed to get to the end of the situation, and only I could do it.

I realized that the hardest job I had to face was to explain everything to my family. The time was ticking away, and I had to make a decision. I decided to take my family to where it all began, in Central Park. It was a beautiful Sunday morning, and everyone was gathering to meet me. They didn't know why, and I wasn't telling them until we all got there. This was the day that all my frustrations of life were coming to an end. I instructed everyone to form a circle and hold hands. They were all completely confused and curious. The anticipation of what I had to tell them was driving them all crazy. I knew I couldn't rush through it. As I stood in the middle of the entire family and watched my grandchildren sitting on the grass, looking up at me, I knew what I was about to say was the best decision of my life. I said, "I love you so much. Today I am faced with a huge decision. My mind is made up, and I just want you to know what is going on…"

I went on to tell them that I had been born in a place called Lavasa. It was a fourth dimension of earth and appeared only to the people who were born there. That was why, for most of my life, I saw through the clouds. I told my family that I was told to go to Central Park, and someone would meet me there, and that's exactly what happened. "I know this sounds unbelievable, but please, just listen," I said. "A woman met me right where we are standing now, and she took me to meet my birth parents. The strangest and most unbelievable thing is that I got to see Frank again. He lives in the land of Lavasa."

Everyone was wondering what they hell I was talking about. Tony walked over to me and hugged and kissed me, like he thought I was going completely crazy at this point. I looked at him and said, "Please, Tony, you must believe me; all of this is true." As I looked at each and every person's face, I began to see fear, and I did not want that to happen.

"This is all true," I said. "I know it may be hard for you to believe, but I am telling the truth." At that very moment, everyone looked stunned as they saw a white horse coming closer and closer. On the horse was a woman. Everyone stood as if they were frozen. She got off the horse, walked over to us, and said, "All of this is true. I am here because I want to meet my real sisters." Francesca and Isabella looked like they saw a ghost as the woman turned to them and began to speak. "Please, do not be afraid. My birth parents are Cosmo and Frances Avellino. I am your sister. I do not want to come here. I want to stay in Lavasa. I just wanted to come and meet my family. Unfortunately for me, my birth parents are gone. However, I can see and sense that they built a good family." She turned to Sofia and said, "You will never see Lavasa again because your decision is made. I only want to come and set the record straight. Sofia is not crazy or overworked. Everything she saw and felt all these years was real. Sofia, now you can rest knowing the truth." She

smiled at everyone and walked away, seeming to disappear among the cherry blossoms. No one uttered a
sound. I started to cry.

I said, "After all is said and done, I know there is no
place for me but here with all of you whom I adore and
love, who hold the key to my heart. I could never walk
away. I was taken to Lavasa. I met everyone I needed
to meet, and they are wonderful, warm, loving people.
However, they are not my family. You are, and I am not
leaving. I got to meet the real Sofia Avellino, as you just
did. She, like me, does not want to leave her home. She
wants to stay in Lavasa with the loves of her life that she
has created in the last fifty years.

"Yes, I was kidnapped as a baby. Mama did not know
I had been switched. It wasn't until many years later that
she received a phone call and was told the truth about
me. Right before she passed away, Mama gave me a book
that held the secrets of my life, and I was finally able to
find out the truth I never knew. I saw and felt things differ-
ently from other people because I am different from other
people. It turns out that there are many people on earth
from Lavasa, the city in the clouds. They are also faced
with this most difficult decision. As for me, I am never
leaving my sons, my grandchildren, all of you, my family—
you are my life. I am so glad I solved this crazy, mixed-up
story about Sofia.

"I thank God that I am here with my family. The mystery is finally over. I am Sofia Avellino from Park Avenue,
daughter of Cosmo and Frances, sister of Francesca and

Isabella, and mother of Marcello, Joseph, and Cosmo, and I am staying this way. All of this will go to rest forever and ever."

As tears flooded my eyes, I couldn't see straight anymore. I continued, "I am thrilled that this journey is over. I know what real love and life are all about. It's right here with all of you, and I will never take it for granted."

As I said all these words, I was still confident in my decision. I knew I could never walk away from Marcello's beautiful smile, Joseph and his striving for perfection, and Cosmo with his overwhelming zest for life.

"All three of you keep me going, and I'd have no life if I left you. My sisters, daughters-in-law, my entire family, and of course, my grandchildren. And you, my darling, Tony. You have stood by my side through thick and thin and have given me a life as if I live over the rainbow. Nothing but sunshine, love, and passion, and where I am today is because of our love. I refuse to leave earth, and therefore I will never see Lavasa in the clouds again. I intend to be here for a loving, caring, wonderful journey, now that I know who Sofia Avellino really is.

One year later...

———— ❧ ————

TIME DOES HEAL all wounds. My parents are gone, and we are all here, surviving and doing very well. The boys are running the business with perfection. Mama and Papa will rest in peace knowing they did a good job and their legacy will live on with their children and grandchildren.

As for me, I often wander in Central Park. I take a seat on a bench and stare up at the sky and I try to find the clouds that once revealed my home. I know I made the right decision. I could never live happily without my life in New York and my family by my side. If only I knew more about Lavasa. I admit, it tugs at my heart, not knowing my birth parents. I do wish Lavasa gave me more time to learn about that place in the clouds. Did I make a mistake? Imagine living in a stress-free world. No crime, no terror, no poverty, no cancer, no bills—nothing like we're used to. Yes, I would have lived with Frank, my first husband. I often wonder, *Would I have survived?* I know he was hurt and disappointed when I told him that I could not leave the earth. In any decision in life, someone usually gets hurt; that is just how life is.

Now, I fly and look for those clouds that haunted me for so many years, and all I see is the blue sky. The images

I saw my entire life are gone, I will never see them again. Sometimes, in the silence of the night, I miss all that. It is very odd, and yes, very strange. My life is here, and who knows? Maybe at the end of my life, they will come for me. No one really did explain it all to me. I was so scared and afraid of all that I had to deal with, I just wanted the comfort of my life here in the city. So now, I sit and day-dream about what could have been. I'm not unhappy that I'm here. Yes, I do feel bad about not knowing my birth parents. After all, I'm not really an Avellino and maybe not even Italian. No one told me my real name.

Our family is still working hard in our business, and everyone is constantly busy. No one talks about that day in Central Park when they learned the truth about Sofia. It is as if it never happened. It seems to be taboo. My children do not want to hear it; they say that as far as they are concerned, I am their mother, it is here that I belong, and that is final.

The
End

…or is it just the beginning?

Frank John Azzinaro

My father was a man for all seasons, honest and so loyal. He worked hard for his family, never even missing a day of work. Together, he and my mother gave us a happy life. Having served in the United States Army during World War II, he was a true American and was devoted to his country. His nickname was "the Colonel."

I loved writing about my parents; it was a wonderful feeling, reliving the memories. Once you lose your parents, life is never the same. It's only then that you realize how much you have lost.

Rest in peace, dear Papa. Until we meet again.

Your oldest daughter,

Margaret

Frances Marie Billera Azzinaro

This page in my book is for my mother. To this typical Italian, old-fashioned lady, cooking, cleaning, and serving her family were all that mattered. She worked from the moment she got up until the moment she went to bed, making sure her home was like a dollhouse. From the time we were little, Mom taught my sisters and me that family always comes first. My mom lost her battle to breast cancer twenty years ago. As I wrote *The Beautiful Life of Sofia*, I brought her memories back, and it felt extraordinary.

Mom, you are forever in my heart. As I approach my twentieth year of being a survivor, I think of you daily.

Rest in peace, my dear mother. Loving you always.

Meet the Real Avellino Sisters

From left to right: Margaret, Cecilia, and Elizabeth

Photo by Maria Billera-Amaro

About the Author

Margaret Azzinaro-Bonacci lives an amazing life in Brooklyn, New York, with the man who holds the key to her heart. Together they share five sons and six wonderful grandchildren. This book is parallel to her real Italian lifestyle. Margaret is no stranger to being in the  public eye. She represented New York in the Mrs. New York State/Mrs. America pageant. She continued this path by running pageants for young beauties in the Little Miss Brooklyn and Little Miss Italy pageants. During those events, Margaret shared a stage with many famous directors, radio personalities, councilmen, and former New York Mayor Ed Koch.

One of the highlights of her life was when President Ronald Reagan presented an award to her for heroic actions. Margaret has also been on the stage, TV, and radio with her acting and speaking talents. You might say she has done it all. She is currently employed by NYPD. Her life is full of happiness, love, and hope. Being a breast-cancer survivor, she loves life and appreciates each and every day.